CLAIM

SIENNA SNOW

CHAPTER ONE
Sophia

"YOU ARE THE lady with all the connections. I'm so glad we keep you around." Farah Lance, a fellow model at my agency, slurred as she tried to lift a bottle of champagne to her fire engine red-stained lips and danced without toppling over.

Shaking my head, I leaned back on a plush sofa in the VIP section of the Stingers Lounge, an exclusive new hot spot near Hell's Kitchen in New York City.

"Don't you mean it's a good thing she lets you tag along on her escapades at all the elite parties with all the celebrities she knows?" Christo, another of the models with us, asked.

"I say it's a fair trade since I brought her into the group when she first came onto the scene."

I took a healthy swallow of my sparkling water disguised as vodka with soda and stood. "Considering this was over eight years ago, we can call that debt paid in spades. According to my assessment, you owe me for all the times we've ended up on the society pages because of my invite-only experiences."

"She's got you there, Farah. That table incident got you that campaign for the denim line."

"See. Chris proved my point." Plucking an olive from a martini a server brought to our table, I popped it into my mouth.

I scooted around the two as they continued discussing what I owed to whom.

The Met Gala after-party bar incident had garnered Farah a lucrative contract. Whereas I'd dealt with weeks upon weeks of criticism from the press, the elite of Bishop's Landing society, and most of all, my family, namely my parents. The sad part of the incident was that I'd never gotten on top of the bar. I'd held Farah's hand as she climbed up so she wouldn't fall, but someone caught a photo and posted it online. Therefore, everyone assumed I'd joined her for the antics.

Oh well. Maybe next time, I'd join Farah and give the gossip rags something real to report on.

Not a chance.

The idea of that appealed to me as much as scheduling a dental visit. Being a tabloid darling once upon a time helped me feel something.

Now, it felt like another duty to fulfill as part of my to-do list.

Pick and wear the latest up-and-coming designer's creation – check.

Score an invitation to the latest and greatest event in town – check.

Meet the right people – check.

Have photographs taken by the right media outlets – check.

Avoid falling into another tabloid-worthy scandal – the jury was still out on this one.

Number five on my list was something I tried to adhere to constantly. For the most part, I'd succeeded in my endeavors. The Farah incident occurred more than a year ago, which was a record in my book. But no matter how hard I tried to avoid it, trouble seemed to find me.

Or, as my mother would surely tell me, "Trouble follows the wicked, Sophia."

And in her eyes, I was most definitely wicked and living a life of sin.

Strolling through the other patrons in the VIP section, I smiled at a few of the celebrities in-house that I passed and then made my way to the bar to refill my mocktail.

That's when I heard, "God, look at that dress. By wearing it, she's only reminding everyone here that she's his whore."

I stiffened, knowing the voice belonged to a catty bitch, who hated my guts. I'd called out her elite circle of friends for ganging up on a fifteen-year-old model who'd gotten a coveted spot in the lineup at a fashion show.

Bullies hated when someone, as vicious as they were, confronted them about their shitty behavior. However, since that day, this group had gone out of their way to poke at me if they were in the vicinity.

The best way to handle them was to pretend they didn't exist.

I approached the bartender and leaned in. "Vodka soda, minus the vodka."

"Coming up." The guy grinned as I passed him a twenty.

And then they tried it again. "How many designers has she gone through? Five or six. Does she fuck all of them?"

"It's not the designers she's into. It's the jewelers."

"No, I heard she's banging the lead singer of that band."

"She's such a TMZ wannabe. Always doing something to get attention. She should get on a table like Farah if she's so desperate to get a contract."

They all started laughing, and the last comment was so loud that I knew nearly every group around them had heard the words that had me clenching my jaw.

These assholes knew nothing about me, and to spread shit like that was aggravating. They had no clue what it was like being a Morelli, to have things like that get back to my family.

I'd dealt with this most of my adult life. Slut shaming someone, knowing that they'd been the one to do wrong, was the lowest of the low.

The damage, the pain, and as a whole what it does to a person's life.

Turning, I stalked over to the group. I pushed past two large guys and got in the face of a tall blonde.

"Tabatha, did you say something about my love life?"

The shock in her gray eyes would have amused me if I wasn't ready to punch her.

"I have no idea what you're talking about. We were discussing clothing."

"Listen very carefully. If you don't have the lady balls to admit the gossip you spread about people to their face, I suggest shutting the fuck up."

She narrowed her eyes and glared at me. "What about you?"

"I own what I say. You are a lying asshole who can't admit when you're in the wrong. I—" I took a step toward her, ready to cause a tabloid-worthy scene for which I'd happily accept the consequence with my family.

That was when my gaze caught the silhouette of a man I'd know anywhere, and my stomach dropped, and bile threatened to rise in my throat.

I hated that bastard with every fiber of my being.

I'd barely stepped out of my childhood when he'd cost me more than I wanted to admit.

Why was he here?

I'd gone out of my way to ensure he wasn't on the guest list.

Why wouldn't he leave me alone?

He'd taken so much from me already.

I had to get out of here.

Keep it together, Sophia.

Gathering my thoughts, I focused on Tabatha and spoke without revealing my unease, "I don't have time for you and your petty antics. You know damn well I'm not with anyone, and I have this dress because I bought it."

"Not all of us have daddy's money to pay our

bills."

"True. I'm fortunate. But my money paid for this ensemble, not my daddy's. I work, or did you miss that I'm the face of three lucrative campaigns?"

Turning, I walked away as fast as my heels would allow without losing my balance.

I kept my gaze forward, not daring to risk seeing the smug satisfaction on the bastard's face at seeing me leave a party because of him.

There was no point in going back to my table. Farah and Christo were used to me bailing, knowing I rarely stayed for a whole evening. They'd inform the rest of our crew.

I needed to add a number six to my list of to-dos: Avoid the asshole at all costs.

It was another thing I mostly accomplished. Because of him, I'd turned into this girl. I'd hardened myself. I built walls. I let others believe what they wanted about me. As a result, I'd lost the essence of Sophia Donatella Morelli.

Fuck it.

I knew where I had to go, someplace where I felt free, or at least some semblance of free.

Taking the steps toward the exit, I texted my driver, telling him my destination.

No more voyeur for me. No more fascination

with the lifestyle that called to me. No more fear of exploring what lurked inside me.

I planned to live in the moment.

Now, I only had to find the right someone to introduce me to the many facets of this new territory.

CHAPTER TWO

I STUDIED MY reflection in the mirror across from me one last time, giving my face a once over from all angles and then stepping back.

There was freedom in the exchange of control. Of power. Or so I'd heard.

I wouldn't know, as I lived a life playing on a knife's edge.

The wild child, the party girl, the disappointment no one could bring to heel. Those were the terms used to describe me.

Who was Sophia Donatella Morelli?

With any luck, I'd find out tonight. No matter what, I'd keep searching until I discovered the girl hidden deep inside me and set her free. I'd tell her she was safe and could be herself without consequences.

Wasn't that why I'd gone to my brother Lucian's club? Why I stood here in one of Violent Delights' dressing rooms, preparing to join the patrons of the establishment?

This club called to something in me. It was a

hedonistic and strictly forbidden space reserved for those with certain mindsets and varying palates of desires. I relished my time here, whereas I'd despised every second spent at the Stingers Lounge.

I smoothed out the silk accents on the form-fitting bustier I'd custom-designed to fit the curves of my body and adjusted the garter belts and stocking on my thighs.

If my mother saw me in this, would it scandalize her? Or would she shake her head and wonder where she'd gone wrong with me?

More than likely, the latter.

Sarah Morelli had given up on me a long time ago. She'd rather believe the worst than come to me even once and ask if any of the rumors about me were true. When in all actuality, the things posted about me were purely fabricated ninety-nine percent of the time.

I embodied the black jewel nestled among her sea of pure white diamonds. She'd never believe that I was probably the most innocent of her precious daughters. But, then again, the perceptions about me became a reality when one was the nonconformist in the Morelli household. I'd rather push back than continually have my voice silenced.

Shake it off, Sophia. This wasn't the time for a pity party.

Turning, I closed my eyes for the briefest moments to release all the tension in my body. Finally, after a few breaths, I had my confidence firmly in place and stepped out of the door.

An air of dripping sensuality engulfed me as I walked down one of the private hallways decorated in rich splashes of blues, maroons, and shades of gold.

Tonight, I planned to enjoy, watch, and forget about anything the outside world believed about me. I wasn't Sophia Morelli. I was just a masked woman exploring.

Who was I kidding?

As Lucian's sister, I couldn't disappear here even if I tried. And I'd tried, even going as far as to wear a wig and colored contacts on my first visit. But my status as the owner's sibling came out to the club patrons before I'd stepped into the lounge.

I'd considered visiting other clubs but decided against it. No matter how hard I tried, my celebrity status posed a risk I couldn't shed.

At least here, I was safe.

I wouldn't have to worry about tabloids, gossip, photographs, or invasion of my privacy.

There were ways to protect myself, but sometimes not having to stay on alert was a nice change of pace.

Over the years, I'd let my guard down too many times, only to regret it later.

Plus, I knew Lucian preferred that I explore things about myself in the walls of his club versus someone else's.

I know what he would do—to anyone who dared to cross the line when it came to me.

Using the word unhinged when describing his temper wouldn't do him justice.

Thank God he no longer monitored the club every night. He preferred to spend time at home with his wife, Elaine, and their children. No little sister wanted to venture into their older brother's kink club and then run into said big bro there or even worse, have him witness her first foray from spectator to participant.

I entered the vast expanse of the lounge. Immediately, my skin prickled with awareness, and energy pulsed all around me. The strategic placement of unique furniture and styling gave the area the ambiance of multiple rooms. Allowing a variety of groups to mingle and relax without feeling they were right on top of each other.

A shiver slid down my spine, and my skin prickled as if a predator watched me.

This never happened any of the other three times I'd visited the club. Then again, I'd never wanted to experience the pleasure available here to this level. Those other times, I enjoyed watching and losing myself in the beauty of the public scenes. They drew me and pulled at a part of me I rarely allowed free.

However, tonight there was something, this unexplainable urgency, to delve into the world firsthand.

Maybe the mix of what happened earlier in the evening with the need to feel something other than the expectations drove me.

To lose myself for one night before returning to my everyday life of being a persona non grata.

I scanned the room, noticing a few stares in my direction, but none connected with the sensations currently stirring inside me.

That this unknown feeling aroused me more than scared me made no damn sense.

A cocktail. That's what I needed—something to take the edge off. Then I'd figure out what had riled my senses.

Strolling to the bar in the far corner of the room, I slipped onto a barstool.

"Welcome back, gorgeous." The handsome blond bartender, Tate, said.

He gave me a dazzling smile, setting a cocktail napkin in front of me.

"Dirty martini with extra olives, am I correct?" He set a martini glass on the prep station and waited for my answer.

"You remembered. I'm impressed."

He winked. "That's my job. I have to keep all the beautiful ladies happy."

"Is that right? And it wouldn't have to do with me being the boss's sister?"

"Absolutely not. I play no favoritism at all. But I will if you give me the latest celebrity gossip." His sheepish smile had me grinning back at him and relaxing.

The last time I'd visited the club, Tate and I'd spent most of the night sharing stories about our over-the-top encounters with A-listers.

"Honestly, I have nothing new to share. Just the same old, same old."

He lifted a brow before he rested his arms on the bar and then set his chin on his hands. "Don't be coy. Give me something."

"Okay. Umm… You know that tabloid story about the fight for the pre-fashion week events?"

"You mean about the model who found out

her designer boyfriend was sleeping with another model?"

"Yep?"

"All lies. It was a publicity stunt to get people to the fashion show. They are a throuple. Have been one for as long as I can remember."

The shock on Tate's face was almost comical.

"Wow. I can't believe I fell for that. But, you know," Tate paused, tapping his lip. "Now that I think about it. I've seen them all together for years. Well, don't I feel stupid?"

"Now it's your turn. What juicy encounters have you had recently? I know you moonlight at that swank place in Midtown where things get crazy."

His eyes grew wide. "Keep that quiet. I don't want anyone to find out."

"Do you honestly think Lucian doesn't know? Get real." I rolled my eyes. "Come on, give me something. I spilled some tea."

"Fine. First, tell me if you plan to play spectator or participant tonight?"

I lifted a brow at his nosiness, and he matched my stare and waited.

With a sigh, I answered, "It all depends on if I find someone of interest after I peruse the vicinity."

"Well, if you are perusing. Then I wanted to give you the four-one-one on a member." He leaned forward so only I could hear what he had to say.

I followed suit and angled my ear toward him. "I'm listening."

"His name is Damon Pierce." He waited as if expecting some sort of reaction.

I thought for a few moments, scanning my memory. Slowly I pieced it together. Yes, he recently won the American Institute of Architects Gold Medal. He was the go-to man for design work and construction in New York. His most recent project, a living garden high-rise, would open in a few weeks.

Outside of business, I'd never heard anything about him. Which meant he liked his privacy. More than likely, not someone I'd run into with my line of work or lifestyle.

To verify, Tate and I were thinking of the same person. I asked, "Are you talking about the world-renowned architect with a reputation for his unique structural concepts and exorbitant price tags?

"Among other things."

"Meaning?"

"He's the type of Dom every sub needs to

watch herself around."

This pause thing he did every time he made a statement was starting to annoy the hell out of me.

I cocked my head to the side, giving him a frown. "You can't start divulging information and then leave me hanging. Get to the details. Lucian vets all members. He wouldn't let anyone in who breaks his rules."

"It's not my place to know why Mr. Morelli does anything. My information says Mr. Pierce is dangerous and not someone you want for the long term. Play with him, but never let things go further."

Now that sounded ominous. Sometimes hearing gossip was so annoying. It took a lot of effort to decipher the truth among all the embellishments and drama added in by the storyteller. I'd been the subject of so many tales that every time someone recounted an event, the person conveying the incident added their own spin on the circumstances.

"What do you mean dangerous?"

Tate looked to either side of him, ensuring that no one could hear him. "People said he's a murderer."

"You're kidding."

"No, I'm serious. They say his last long-term submissive grew too attached and refused to accept when things ended with them, so he got rid of her."

The idea of someone going to such lengths made me shudder. Wouldn't it have been easier to tell them to get lost or kick them out? There was something very strange about the rumor that I couldn't quite wrap my head around.

"Does that mean he doesn't have a current submissive anymore?"

"Correct. Mr. Pierce occasionally comes in, enjoys his time, and then leaves. Those who play with him know he isn't looking for anything beyond the night. Though they all think they can change his mind." Tate shook his head. "Idiots."

"And they've heard the rumors?"

"It's an open secret here. No matter the danger, he still attracts willing partners for an evening without trying. He draws them like bees to a flower. Outside of the club is where no one mentions it. So either people ignore the rumors, or someone went to great lengths to keep it from the public."

"I would have heard something that salacious considering the circles I run among. I take it Mr. Pierce isn't very outgoing."

"More of the brooding, aloof type. On the rare occasion that he socializes, it's with Mr. Morelli, Mr. Ventana, and the few others in their select circle of friends." Tate stood straight and smiled at the person who'd approached. "Speaking of Mr. Ventana."

I turned to face Clark Ventana, Violent Delight's head of operations.

He gave me a wicked smile that would have made most women melt on the spot.

"I had a feeling you would grace us with your presence tonight. And why am I not surprised you beelined it to the bar?"

Shrugging, I responded with, "A lucky guess."

Describing him as beautiful was an understatement. Clark had an old Hollywood aura about him, with dark blond hair and sky-blue eyes.

His self-assurance and charm drew me in but not in a romantic way. It was more of a friendly or brotherly type of magnetism. Maybe it was because of his relationship with Lucian. Nothing could ever come of it, even if I had been interested in Clark. Lucian was open to many things, except when it came to his friends. He probably wanted to prevent me from ending up with someone as overprotective and crazy as he was.

If only big brother knew I shared some of his unconventional personality traits. But those were my secrets. Along with the multitude of ones I kept under the guise of the party girl the world saw.

"Are you here to observe again, or will you participate?"

I glanced over my shoulder as that prickle from before skidded along the back of my neck. "It all depends on who piques my interests."

"Well then, let me show you around, and you can find out if anyone tickles your fancy."

Knowing my time with Tate was over, I stepped off my stool and tucked my arm into Clark's. "Lead the way, Mr. Ventana."

CHAPTER THREE

Damon

WHO WAS THAT woman on Clark Ventana's arm?

I'd wanted her from the moment I'd set my eyes on her.

She looked like a goddess, with her dark hair styled in a messy bun with little tendrils of curls framing her face and cascading over her shoulders.

She had paused in the entrance near the hallway, scanning the lounge as if utterly oblivious to how she commanded the room's full attention.

My heart had raced, and my cock had stiffened in response to her powerful pull.

Now upon closer inspection, I can see she was fucking breathtaking.

I set my tumbler on the table beside me and stared, imagining how her hair would feel between my fingers as I pushed her down to her knees or made her crawl to me.

She'd ignited a craving unlike anything I'd

experienced before.

I wanted her in a way that made me ache to consume and destroy her. Everything about her screamed sex and submission, and I planned to have more than just a taste.

Those fucking lips were perfect, full, lush. I couldn't wait to hear her pleading and the cries coming from them.

The unique style and edge to her clothes, combined with the confident way she carried herself, projected strength and complete self-assurance.

But I saw through the façade down to the aura of pure innocence lying underneath.

An experienced submissive wouldn't have taken that brief moment to compose herself or to scan the room as if searching for some unknown.

This woman held many secrets, and it would take the strongest of us to tempt her into relinquishing all that pent-up control.

Good thing I sat among those ranks.

I couldn't wait to taste the tears she held so tight within.

I scanned the room from my comfortable spot in the back of the lounge area. The other Doms showered this mystery woman with attention, but their smiles never sparked a glimmer of interest in her deep black eyes. Even her companion, Ventana, the most coveted Dom in the room tonight, couldn't garner anything but a polite smile from her.

A hard woman to impress.

I never found it enjoyable to tame the easy ones anyway.

She reminded me of someone, but I couldn't quite put my finger on it. Those features hidden under the lace mask did nothing to disguise high cheekbones and a stunning face that lay under the material. And those eyes—dark as midnight.

I'd expected her to peruse the main floor or meet up with a group when she'd initially arrived. She'd done neither. Instead, she'd strode in directly to the bar and taken a seat.

She'd wanted some liquid courage as a newcomer to Violent Delights.

Too bad, Ventana had swooped in before she'd finished her conversation with the bartender and received her cocktail.

Good. I preferred my submission given with a clear mind.

The club may allow the one cocktail rule for participants of scenes and more for observers. However, I planned to play and discouraged my companions from partaking in libations. A sip was tolerable, but anything more than that tended to dull the experience.

I picked up my soda, finished the contents of my glass, and continued to observe the enchanting submissive making her rounds in the room with Ventana.

I considered him more on the lines of a social friend—someone to shoot the bull with or catch a game. We knew shit about each other's pasts and on occasion, we discussed business and world events.

He wasn't Lucian Morelli, but he'd do in a pinch.

Though it hadn't passed my notice, he'd avoided me tonight. He'd chosen not to bring over the beauty for an introduction, especially when he'd made a point to meet every other available Dom in the lounge.

Had he kept her away for my sake or hers?

A few of my peers had also noticed from the glances passed in my direction. So, I'd say he'd done it for her benefit.

I clenched my jaw as the familiar pain and guilt seared through my chest.

As if I wasn't aware of the things circulating about me.

And because I refused to give a reaction or

deny anything, I was deemed guilty in everyone's eyes. I'd never take a submissive for my own again. It would only lead to pain for all parties involved.

The best thing for me was to play at Violent Delights. Enjoy the women within the club's walls. Let things start and end in the playrooms, and then walk away. I could pretend to be a different man there, not a man haunted by the past, and for a few hours, I could be happy.

No vulnerabilities, no emotions, no long-term entanglements, no pain.

When the urge called, I picked an experienced submissive who knew the rules and understood what I expected.

Even with all the shit spewed about me, I'd never lacked eager submissives to accompany me for an evening of bliss. They all knew my worth and my skill.

And deep down, every fucking one of them understood Lucian Morelli would never let anyone he couldn't trust through the doors of his establishment.

Lucian Morelli. God, I loved the crazy fucker. He was definitely the man to have at one's back in a tough situation.

Our connection went back over a decade, and

we understood how things played out in the world. For example, first-born sons weren't always the favorite, protecting your family meant some of them may not like us, and walking the straight and narrow wasn't always the best choice.

Who was I kidding? Lucian never walked the path of the righteous.

I released a deep breath and settled my attention back on the beautiful raven-eyed submissive, my planned conquest for the night.

I should stick to my norm of experienced companions and stay away from this innocent, but my blood heated thinking of all the depraved things I'd enjoy doing to her.

Would she cry hot tears when I scored her skin with marks tonight? Would she whimper and thrash for more? She'd beg, I had no doubt. She'd scream in pleasure. And she'd come. I couldn't wait to see her come.

I had no doubt I'd have her tonight.

And since no other Dom in the room had held her attention thus far, I know she wouldn't accept anyone else's offer…but mine.

How she held herself and interacted with the Doms, conveyed deeply ingrained social training, not the kind received through the tutelage of a patient Dominant, but etiquette classes and high society parties.

She came from money. I should have picked up on that from the quality of her clothes alone and definitely the gems she wore on her ears. Black diamonds if I wasn't mistaken.

I couldn't wait to learn what made her so important that she commanded personal introductions from Ventana.

A smile tugged at the corner of my mouth at the disappointment on the enchantress's features when she turned toward Ventana, who waited for her on the periphery of the room. They spoke for a few minutes, and then he lifted her hand for a kiss before they parted ways, walking in opposite directions.

Her trajectory led her in the direction of the bar. The second she slipped back onto her original seat, she began an animated conversation with the bartender, Tate. Whatever they discussed seemed to have eased her disappointment. At the same time, Tate created a dramatic and social media-worthy production of creating her cocktail, garnering the attention of some of the members of the lounge.

As he readied to pour her drink, I rose from my seat and smoothed my shirt.

It was time for me to make my move if I wanted to keep the goddess at the bar clearheaded for all that I had planned for her.

CHAPTER FOUR

Sophia

"A TOTAL BUST, huh?" Tate asked as he poured my martini.

"Thanks for stating the obvious."

"I made it extra strong just to take the edge off your disappointment," Tate smirked and then pulled a jar of olives out, prepping to hand me the drink.

A sadness cascaded over me, showing me how I'd failed at another thing in my life.

"Is this a sign that I expect too much if the most eligible Doms do nothing for me? Maybe something's wrong with me."

I couldn't even explore my sexuality without fucking it up.

"There is nothing wrong with you for being selective. I wish others here were more choosy. They want long term but keep going for the ones who only want short term or commitments that only last the length of a scene." Tate shook his head. "I see their broken hearts coming from a mile away."

"I don't want a relationship. I'm not looking for anything but to feel alive."

"This will make you feel something. I promise." He slid the drink in my direction.

Immediately, I lifted it to my lips, taking a healthy swallow. The alcohol, both cool and refreshing, glided down my throat and calmed me.

Tate definitely mastered the art of making a killer martini.

Sighing, I said, "This hits the spot."

"I'll make you another when you're ready."

"I'd get it ready now. I'm an observer all the way tonight." I set my glass on the counter and swirled the toothpick holding the olives in my cocktail.

Suddenly, the tingling of awareness I'd felt when I'd first entered the club lounge sizzled over my skin, and the hum of energy around me completely shifted.

I peeked to my side and noticed a few of the Dommes and Doms around me studying someone with cool inspection and then inclining their heads. Whoever they looked at had to be a peer among them. At the same time, the submissives displayed a variety of expressions, from apprehension and anticipation to undisguised desire.

"Who is everyone looking at?"

"Remember our conversation earlier about a certain Mr. Pierce?"

"Yes."

"Well, he's—" he stopped talking as his attention shifted behind me. "I believe you've caught his attention."

"Me?"

"Yep."

Hmm. Why hadn't Clark introduced us?

I turned on my stool, and my breath froze in my lungs.

Green eyes, unlike anything I'd ever seen before, seared into mine. A pulsing heat and a tingling awareness spread between my legs and over every inch of my skin.

Dear God. What was happening to me?

The most beautiful faces and charismatic personalities surrounded me in my day-to-day life. And yet none of them ever made me want to this level—as if this stranger held a secret knowledge to all I searched for deep within him.

His gaze held me captive, and I couldn't look away.

My pulse thundered in my ears as if his sheer presence had triggered the urge to kneel deep inside me that I couldn't contain. I licked my lips nervously, but before I could reach for my drink to soothe my parched throat, he shook his head slightly, sending yet another electric jolt through my veins. He held me transfixed and prisoner to his intense emerald irises.

This spell he'd cast over me made no sense. I had no idea why I listened, but I turned away from my cocktail and wanted more of his commands. Was this the thrilling freedom I desired so badly? But how was this freedom when I couldn't move and felt transfixed by his will?

He could be dangerous. The warning blared in the back of my mind.

But when had I ever played it safe or followed the rules? As long as I kept things within the confines of the club, I could remain safe, or so I hoped.

Clark approached him, saying something, but Damon ignored him. His focus trained entirely on me.

Logic screamed at me to run from the predator who'd set his sights on me.

The throbbing deep in my core begged me to let him catch me and experience being his prey.

Then maybe for once in my existence, I'd know what it was to live.

Holding the spell over me, he mouthed, "Stay right there."

He shifted past Clark and maneuvered around groups of people as he set his path toward me.

My breath grew more and more unsteady with every step he took, and my nipples pebbled to hard points.

"You don't have to do anything you don't want to," Tate whispered from behind the counter and then added. "But something tells me you've already decided to play on the wild side."

Before I could respond, Damon approached, taking in everything about me from my face down to my toes and back again.

He offered me his hand. "Damon Pierce."

"Sophia." I slid my palm over his large one, the contact sending a surge of heat into my core.

His lips curved. "Just Sophia?"

"Yes." I matched his smile. "Tonight, I am only Sophia. No one else."

"May I have the privilege of your company this evening, Only Sophia?" He traced his thumb around the skin on the top of my hand, sending shivers up my spine.

"You wouldn't have come over here if you

didn't believe I'd say yes."

"A real gentleman always asks." His eyes were intent on mine as he pulled me closer. "So, do I pass the test, Only Sophia?"

I stood and gazed up at him, feeling my pulse quickening. "Are you truly a gentleman, Mr. Pierce?"

"Only if you want me to be." The corner of his mouth quirked up as his emerald eyes sparkled. "May I have your answer?"

Reckless, Sophia. You're being reckless.

My inner voice yelled at me not to do something so foolish. Still, an irresistible part of me was drawn to this man and wanted to explore whatever he had in store for me. After all, in Lucian's club, what harm could befall me? Everyone knew who I was. I might as well try something daring here than elsewhere.

So, with my heart thundering in my ears, I said, "Yes, Mr. Pierce. I will join you for the evening."

His fingers tightened over mine for a second as something passed over his face and disappeared just as fast. Was it relief or something else? Had he expected a refusal?

"Come with me, and let's see where this night leads us." He lifted my hand to his lips and paused, focusing on my wrist. "You aren't wearing a bracelet."

Shit.

I knew I'd forgotten something. The fact Clark hadn't mentioned it meant he'd expected that I'd sit out as I'd done every other time I'd visited the club.

"I left it in the dressing room."

"Mm-hmm," he replied, his scrutinizing gaze causing my spine to tingle. "Would you mind describing the colors of the bracelet?"

I swallowed, my breath growing more and more uneven. "White with a red stripe."

The various stripes on the bracelets signified the status of the person inside the club. All the black ones belonged to the Dominants, with the stripes in the center indicating their experience level and/or kinks. The same went for submissives, switches, tops, and so forth.

As a complete novice, I bore the red stripe in the center. My usual band was silver with a red stripe, indicating a novice observer but open.

Why I'd chosen white, I wasn't sure. It indicated being submissive, and the last thing I ever wanted to be was submissive to any-damn-body. I refused to fall into the life Mom had trapped herself in, married and under my father's thumb.

"How new are you to this?" Damon asked, his hold firm and his presence engulfing all my senses.

I licked my now parched lips. "Very. I'm exploring. Though, I'm not sure why I picked white. I'm not submissive."

He lifted a brow as if he thought my statement was bullshit. "Are you sure you want to play with me knowing what I am and my experience level?"

He wore a black-on-black wristband. The Master level, indicating kink wasn't a hobby or something to enjoy in passing but an integral part of his life.

He waited for my answer without the weight of pressure, only patience. And I had no doubt he'd let me go if I changed my mind.

And more than likely, that's the reason why I nodded and said, "I'm sure."

He nodded, and I realized he'd asked the question to give me one last out but had known I wouldn't walk away.

He seemed to read me in a way no one else had before.

Without another word, he guided me in front of him, setting his fingers on the hollow of my lower back. His touch sent a wave of anticipative heat up my spine. As if with this man, I'd find something I'd missed all my life tonight.

What was it about Damon Pierce that pulled at me when everything Tate told me should warn me away from him?

"You have a decision to make," he stated, pausing between the playrooms open for public viewing and the semi-private playrooms, where only the club personnel monitored the space.

"Public or private?"

"I get to make a choice?"

"Of course, there is always a choice. A negotiation of limits, a discussion of desires, wants, and needs, and above all else, your level of comfort. These are all things to consider in a power exchange."

"As someone who's never done this, what do you believe is the right answer?"

He lifted my chin with the tip of his finger. "There is no wrong or right answer, Only Sophia. It's a matter of comfort. But if you're asking my opinion. A private setting is a better place for your first scene. You won't get in the right headspace if multiple sets of eyes are on you."

I nodded, and a sense of ease flowed over me.

I had no clue how I'd react to any of this. Better to see this through in private versus the middle of a room full of people.

Then he added, "Plus if I make you come, I doubt you want it on a feed your brother can review later."

My eyes widened. "You knew who I was the whole time?"

He ran a thumb over my lower lip. "Not initially. I put it together after you gave me your name, and I connected the family resemblance."

"And you have no worries about how Lucian will react to this?"

"He isn't part of our equation." The heat in his green irises sent a course of arousal throughout my body, and a flood of heat pooled between my legs.

"Then I guess there is nothing else to discuss."

"Oh, we have things to discuss, but not out here."

We made our way through a dimly lit hallway lined with images of men and women in various poses of pleasure taken by photographers I'd met at a party or two.

I focused in on one with a woman bound with her hands above her head and jeweled clamps on her nipples. A riding crop lay between her breast, and the flush on her face and skin conveyed the impression of post-orgasmic bliss. Her beauty radiated out from the photo, as did her pleasure. It drew me in and made me crave to be her.

Damon's hand settled on my lower back, sliding upward along my spine in a gentle caress. "She's beautiful."

"Yes," I whispered.

"Do you want me to bind you? Or is it the crop that calls to you?"

Something about him made it easy to tell him the truth. "It's the whole essence of the scene. It makes me wonder what it would feel like to be her."

"I can give you that. Albeit without the clamps."

"Why omit the clamps?" Curiosity had me asking the question.

I'd read enough about them to know the bit of them caused a stinging pain before euphoria set in. It required a slow integration to enjoy the pleasure of it.

"It isn't a beginner device. I'd have to train you into it."

I turned to face him, ready to ask him what he meant by train, but my words never materialized as he collared my throat.

The comforting pressure shouldn't feel so good, so delicious, so needed.

"Let's go in the room." He reached around me and opened the door.

His hold on my neck remained firm, unyielding but not painful, and he walked me inside.

"Now, we discuss your limits."

"I don't know what they are."

"Are you truly so innocent, Only Sophia? Have you never played games with any of your lovers?"

I wanted to look away, hide from his probing eyes, and keep my secrets buried.

"No, I'm not innocent."

I'd seen more than enough of how the world worked.

The good, the bad, and the dirty.

"Then tell me, what won't you do?"

I thought for a moment about what I knew of the kink world. "No blood, knives, the rest, I'll say, if we cross it."

He nodded. "What is your safe word?"

"Marriage," slid from my lips before I gave it a second thought.

He cocked his head to the side, studying me. I wanted to respond, defend my choice, and tell him not every girl had dreams of white picket fences and two-point-five children, but I kept my thoughts to myself.

Then as if he accepted my choice, he gestured to the table in the center of the room. "Have a seat on the end. We have to finish our conversation."

Immediately my pulse jumped, but I found myself following his command. Once situated on the table covered in plush leather, I waited.

He approached, setting a hand on either side of me. "Only Sophia, don't look so worried. I'm not a tyrant. All I expect is honesty at all times. Never take more than you can bear. Your safe word is there for a reason. Do you understand?"

"Yes." Then I asked, "What do I call you?"

"I thought you said you weren't a submissive?"

I frowned. "I'm not. I'm exploring. And there are still rules."

His face loomed closer to mine, and I couldn't help but sway closer. "Well, Only Sophia, the explorer. You call me Damon. I'm not one for honorifics."

"It can't be that simple. You have to have other rules."

He smiled, sending a flutter into my stomach, then listed things he expected, all of which were standard in the world of kink.

However, when he said, "And each time you

don't listen, expect consequences."

I asked, "What do you mean by consequences?"

Though the thought of the unexpected intensified the throbbing between my legs.

"You'll find out soon enough." He leaned forward. "Now to the most important rule."

My breath grew unsteady as my nipples beaded.

"You can't come unless I give you permission."

He'd lost his mind if he believed I had any control over it.

As if reading my thoughts, he answered, "Oh, you can do it. Remember, the reward is well worth the wait."

I licked my lips and swallowed, trying desperately to ease my now parched mouth.

"One last question before we begin."

I knew what he planned to ask. I sensed it deep in my bones. If I agreed, he'd know the first of my secrets: I lived a lie. But then again, someone would know I wasn't what everyone believed.

"Intercourse. Yes or no?"

I stared at him, my breath growing unsteady, uncertainty warring with desire for this stranger.

He traced a finger along my jaw. "There is no right or wrong answer. I don't need to come to make you come. This is about you. In a power exchange, the submissive holds the true power."

I opened my mouth to argue and remind him I wasn't a submissive, but I found myself saying, "Yes."

"Now we begin, Only Sophia Morelli." He brushed a soft, caressing kiss over my temple, a gesture I hadn't expected. "Let's explore your very submissive side."

As he stepped back, he brought an eye mask into view and slipped it over the one I already wore. "I believe it's better for you to feel rather than see."

Darkness engulfed me, and my senses fired to life. The room's scent became more intense, the coolness of the air prickled my skin, the way the cushioning on the table pressed against my thighs felt more pronounced, and the heady energy pulsing from the man standing before me gave me the sensation of light-headedness.

"Let yourself fall into it," Damon coached. "Trust that I have you."

My skin tingled, and deep in my slick pussy the aching need grew. My heartbeat accelerated, drumming in an erratic rhythm.

Trust, he said. Trust. How could I trust him when I only truly relied on myself?

A tremor shook my body, and a pang of fear settled inside me.

This was too fast, too soon.

"What is happening to me?" I reach out, needing to grasp onto something.

Damon captured my wrists, setting them on his chest. "Breathe. Do you ever release control, Only Sophia?"

I fisted his shirt as a sense of calm settled over me. His heat seeped into my fingers, and the pressure of his hands on me soothed the jagged edges that constantly reminded me I had to protect myself.

Finally, when my emotions settled, I answered, "No. People take advantage if you do. Trust isn't something I can afford to give anyone."

"For tonight, give it to me. I promise you won't regret it."

I believed him. Why? I couldn't explain it.

I just knew that I felt safe at this moment to relinquish the tight hold I kept on myself.

And the fact he'd centered me, given me comfort, and remained patient when I panicked told me I could trust him.

Well, for this moment, at least.

Taking a centering breath, I said, "Tonight, only."

CHAPTER FIVE

Damon

"BREATHE," I COAXED, staring down at Sophia's flushed face.

"I'm trying. This is all new to me."

The area covering her eyes showed a small patch of dampness, revealing that she'd shed a few tears.

I fucking loved tears.

This vulnerability called to me better than any siren song.

Was this woman as innocent as she seemed, or was it all part of the shield she wore?

My gut warned that the true her sat before me now, and the impostor was the one she showed the world.

So pure, so unsure, so ready to explore. She had no clue who she was.

The thought of corrupting her, molding her to my wants and desires, pulled at that deep seeded need I'd locked away.

But only an idiot would walk away from introducing her to the world of kink.

Later, I'd pay the consequences of touching Lucian's sister. But, right now, the draw to her was too intense to deny.

I cupped her flushed face, running my thumb along the skin exposed under her mask.

"Are you ready to explore, Only Sophia?"

Her skin prickled with goosebumps. "Yes."

"We'll go slow." I took hold of her wrists as they gripped my shirt as if it were a lifeline and pulled her forward.

Her breathing became erratic when she stood before me as if uncertainty overwhelmed her. No matter how much I wanted to push her to drop her guard, I wouldn't force her into anything she wasn't ready to experience.

I craved absolute control, and this wouldn't work unless she gave it to me.

"You can change your mind, and we can return to the lounge."

She shook her head, and she stepped closer to me. "No. I need to know why I'm drawn to this."

"Our scene has officially started." I threaded my fingers into her long hair, tilting her head back. "As of this point, the only way to stop things is to use your safe word. What is your word?"

"Marriage." She licked her lips.

"I'm going to test two objects on you and then place them in your hands. Whichever one you offer me is the instrument I will use on you tonight."

Her hold on my shirt tightened, and she shifted slightly. "Okay."

"You must let go of me for our scene to commence." I brought my face a fraction toward hers, letting my stubble graze her cheek.

She turned into my touch, and then her fingers eased their grip as we both released each other and stepped back.

The wild child of the Morellis, so beautiful and completely out of her element. No bright lights or runways or A-list parties. Only a Dom who planned to teach her things she never knew she wanted.

The play of emotions on her face told a story of a woman who may own her sexuality in public but had never experienced true release or freedom.

Her lips parted, taking in an unsteady breath, and immediately I had visions of sliding my cock into that perfect full mouth of hers, of seeing beautiful tears soak through that red mask as she took me all the way back and struggled to handle my thrusts.

"Damon," her whisper of my name had me snapping out of my fantasy and moving to a set of cabinets in the back corner of the room.

I selected a paddle and flogger. One end of each item had a hard handle wrapped in leather, constructed to allow the user control. On the other end was where they differed.

The flogger consisted of a multitude of long buttery soft leather tendrils designed to give a beautiful glow and bite to a submissive's skin without causing excessive abrasions. The paddle was made of smooth cherry wood, thin and flat on two sides.

Before I brought them to her, I knew which one she'd pick.

The flogger.

The very little interaction I'd had with her told me she craved to lose complete control. And that required pain, not just in a centralized location.

With the flogger, I could work her whole body.

Moving behind her, I trailed both instruments along the outer edges of her thighs, making her shiver.

"Hold out your hands."

I struck the paddle down into her palm as soon as she followed directions.

"Oh." she jerked, curling her fingers for a moment before stretching them out again, and then she waited, anticipating the strike to the other hand.

Giving her what she expected, I smacked the flogger onto her skin.

She flinched, but this time she kept the gasp inside.

A deep blush crept up the column of her neck, and she lifted her arm as if requesting more.

It looked as if I'd made the correct assessment.

Moving in front of her, I set the handles of the flogger and the paddle in each of her palms.

"Two different instruments of pleasure with unique sensations and experiences to discover. Both can push you if done well. One will take you further faster. How far do you want to go, Only Sophia?"

Without a second's hesitation, she wrapped her fingers around the hilt of the flogger and offered it to me. "All the way, Damon Pierce."

Heat filled her dark gaze, and the confidence I'd seen when she'd entered the lounge had returned in full force.

Interesting.

The uncertainty of moments earlier had disappeared, and she'd won whatever battle plagued her mind.

Was it the flogger that snapped her out of it?

Whatever it was, it looked as if she was ready to explore.

"All the way, is it? It all starts with following orders." I waited for a few heartbeats and then commanded. "Strip."

A smile touched her lips, and she asked, "Is the mask part of the stripping?"

The tinge of humor in her question had me shaking my head.

Of course, Sophia Morelli fell into the category of a brat.

"Keep it on. It's part of the experience. Pretend you're preparing to walk the runway. I'm sure you don't even notice if anyone sees your naked body there."

She pursed her lips for a quick second before she schooled the emotions away, making me realize I'd treaded onto a tender subject. So she wasn't as free with her body as it would seem.

"Then is it everything except for my mask?"

"Leave your underwear but take off everything else."

Without another word, she removed her

clothing bit by bit, hesitating every so often before inhaling deeply and then continuing.

The enigma of this woman confused the hell out of me. One second she oozed pure feminine self-assurance, and the next, a vulnerable innocence made me want to protect her and keep her safe from the world.

The craving to dive into the deepest part of her and peel back all of the layers until I understood why she pretended to be so many different things all at the same time pushed at every fiber of my being.

Neither of us could afford to cross that line. This was not only due to the cost to our respective relationships with Lucian but to the toll a claim meant to our lives.

She knew nothing about the devil she played with tonight.

The facts or fiction of the rumors about me were all relative based on the person telling the story. My ability to engulf a submissive's senses during a scene was legendary in the club. The patrons could only imagine what a submissive I took for my own would feel. Therefore, no matter what, I accepted that I was guilty for what happened.

Now here I was, watching this goddess strip

and reveal her tall and slim model's body. Well, except for that curvy ass, which wasn't typical runway material at all. Those were beautiful Italian genetics at their best.

I couldn't wait to see her skin glow red with my marks or hear her cries.

When she was bare except for her tiny thong, I moved behind her, setting my hand on her waist.

Immediately, goosebumps prickled her skin. Then, leaning down, I grazed my stubble along the column of her neck, and a low whimper escaped her lips.

So responsive, and we'd barely started.

I walked her toward the padded table where she had previously sat and turned her, putting her voluminous ass against it. "I'm going to lay you back. You will hold onto the bar at the top. Your job is to hold on tight without letting go, no matter what I do to you."

Her breath came out in unsteady pants as I positioned her the way I stated, and her nipples pebbled to stiff peaks, making them a distracting temptation for my plans.

"Are you ready, Only Sophia?"

She nodded.

"I need the words."

"Yes."

Slowly I circled the table, letting the leather threads of the flogger tease her skin. I started trailing up her arms, over her shoulders, across her neck, down her stomach, along her thighs, between her fabric-covered center and then back to where I'd started.

I lulled her into a trance to give her comfort and keep her mind from worrying or making up too many scenarios. This way when I brought the flogger down, she'd get the greatest impact of that first bite of the leather tendrils.

Smack.

"Oh, dear God," she gasped, arching up but not releasing her hold on the bar above her.

The blush on her thigh so beautiful was only the beginning.

"Do you want more?"

"Y-yes." She bit her lip as her chest lifted up and down.

With slow, measured strikes, I worked her legs, thighs, arms, and abdomen.

"Please." The way she kept raising her breast, I knew she was begging for some attention there, but I wasn't ready to give in to her demands just yet.

"What do you want?"

"I don't know. Something. Please. It feels as if I'll die if I don't get it. Just do it." She squirmed and pressed her thighs together as if it would give her the relief she desired.

Who would have believed a princess like her enjoyed pain and depraved cravings?

She cried out as I pushed her legs apart, stepping between them, refusing to allow her any reprieve from her discomfort.

"Asshole."

Ignoring her ire, I focused on the arousal pooling between her legs. It called to me in a way no dessert had before.

I grabbed hold of her thong and ripped it from her body. "I doubt you'll call me that in a few seconds."

"What are you going to do?"

The way she stiffened had me looking up at her, but since she still held onto the bar, this was just her curiosity pushing her to ask.

"You'll have to wait and see." Dropping to my knees, I brought my mouth a hairsbreadth to her sweet, soaked pussy. "Well, you can't see, can you? You'll just have to experience, Only Sophia. That's why you're here, after all."

I descended on her, worrying her sensitive bundle of nerves and gorging on her sopping cunt. She cried out and whimpered. Her hips thrashed and bucked. However, all the while, she never released the bar above her head.

When her orgasm washed over her, the scream she released was complete music to my ears.

I wiped my mouth on her inner thigh and rose. A lesser man would bury himself in her right now, but we were far from done. I had yet to make her come from just the flogger.

"Are you ready to really begin now, Only Sophia?"

"W-what have we been doing all of this time?"

"Foreplay."

CHAPTER SIX

Sophia

*F*OREPLAY.

He had to be kidding.

My mind whirled as I'd barely come down from my first non-self-administered orgasm.

Need and arousal continued to course throughout my system, and the ache deep inside my core seemed to have grown by leaps and bounds.

I hadn't expected to enjoy this so much, and now I wasn't sure if I could walk away from wanting to experience this over and over again.

But would he want to do this with me again?

Sophia, enjoy this one night before you jump too far ahead of yourself.

"Should I be scared?"

"Are you scared?"

Was I?

I shook my head. "No. For some reason, I feel safe with you."

"I'm the worst thing that can happen to you, Only Sophia."

His ominous words sent a shiver down my spine, but it also called to that defiant part of me to cross the lines that told me no, or you shouldn't do it.

"I'll take my chances."

"You are a brat, Sophia Morelli."

"I've been called so many worse things. Brat is tame by comparison."

"Brat isn't an insult." Damon took hold of my wrists, bringing them down from the bar above my head, and rubbed the muscles from my shoulders to my hands. "It's your temperament as a submissive."

An irritation prickled in the back of my mind, and without a second thought, I responded with, "I'm not submissive."

"I know, you're exploring." He made no attempt to hide the amusement in his tone. "Let's explore your not-so-submissive side some more."

He brought my hands down and then bound them with two straps. "I want you to hand over complete control. Whether you could let go or not. This scene, I control everything."

"Can I lose the mask?"

"Why?"

"I don't want to feel as if I'm with a stranger. I want to see your face."

He trailed his fingers up my torso, making me shiver. Then I felt his breath glide over my lips.

"Did it feel like I was a stranger when I was fucking you with my mouth?" He pushed the blindfold and my lace mask from my face.

I kept my eyes closed, knowing it would take a few moments to let them adjust to the change in light. Then, slowly, I opened them and focused on Damon's blazing green gaze.

"I knew it was you, but..." I trailed off, unsure how to phrase what I wanted to say.

"But?"

Swallowing the lump in my throat, I answered, "I feel this intensity when I look into your eyes. I want to experience it during the scene."

"Are you sure you can keep your gaze on me as we play? That takes discipline. The pain and pleasure are very intense."

Was he throwing down a challenge?

Lifting my chin, I pursed my lips and said, "You'll break before I do."

"You are definitely not what I expected to encounter when I came into the club tonight." His slight smile had me responding in kind. "Let's begin."

He stood, walked over to where he'd placed the flogger, took it in his hand, and then returned to me. Then, holding my stare, he let the first strike land.

I gasped but kept my eyes trained on his emerald ones. Tears blurred my vision as heat penetrated my skin and coursed down into my pussy. The exquisite sensation burned through my mind, and I couldn't wait for more.

"More."

"You like pain?"

"Yes," I gasped.

"Good. I enjoy giving it to you. Now give me those beautiful tears."

Over the next few minutes, he worked every inch covering the front of my body, except my breasts and pussy. The two very areas I needed the leather threads to score with teasing fingers of pain.

"Please," I begged, unable to do anything else.

He held my gaze as he rotated the handle in graceful circles with his wrist and struck the sides of my breasts over and over. "Is this what you want?"

"Yes. God, yes." I arched up, forcing myself not to close my eyes and lose myself in the euphoria of the pleasure-filled torment. "More.

I'm almost there."

"Do you feel the urge to come, Sophia?" He struck the juncture of my crotch, purposely missing my pussy. "Does your cunt ache for something to fill it?"

The bastard. I couldn't take this anymore. The ache, the need.

He had to do something, more pain, more something to send me over.

"Stop torturing me and make me come." I jerked at my restraints as tears poured down my cheeks.

Suddenly, Damon dropped the flogger and loomed over me, bringing his face over mine. "I don't take orders from you. I'm in charge. You orgasm when I give you permission."

A hiccup escaped my lips, and I couldn't help the sobs that erupted from my throat.

"Do you know how beautiful you look, crying as you are? It makes me so hard, Only Sophia. I want to fuck you for hours and make you weep even more. You're a fucking goddess."

The knot in my belly fisted so tight I could barely breathe, and the desperation I felt for relief was unlike anything I'd experienced.

"I don't like crying. It means I'm weak, that I'm vulnerable."

"You are the furthest thing from weak. There is strength in lowering your guard with the right person. I won't use them against you."

More tears spilled from the corners of my eyes. With this man, it felt freeing, as if I'd found a safe space to release all the pent-up emotions I'd held in since my late teens.

He rubbed his lips over mine, nipping at them. "Do you want to come, Only Sophia?"

Oh God, he had to send me over or I'd go mad with want.

"Damon. Please. I'll do anything."

"What is it you'll give me?" He slid his fingers between my pussy lips, stroking my clit and making me buck up into his touch. "Right now, you'd give the devil your soul for this orgasm."

Using his thumb, he circled my clit and then pushed two fingers in and out of my channel in shallow thrusts. It was a wicked tease meant to drive up my desire even more.

Bastard.

I pushed my heels onto the table's edge and lifted my hips, trying to get more penetration, but he pulled out.

"Naughty girl. That's not how this works. But since you've put yourself on display for me. Keep yourself just like that."

My eyes widened when he picked up the flogger, and before I could open my mouth, he flicked the leather tendrils between my splayed thighs.

My scream locked in my throat as fire, agony, and complete bliss shot through my clit and pussy.

"Don't you dare look away," he ordered.

I could do nothing but follow his command as his piercing, lust-filled green irises held me prisoner. Air finally filled my lungs, and I gasped and wailed in pleasure and pain, letting the earth-shattering release cascade through my body. Then, my mind clouded, and a sensation of floating engulfed me.

Pure unadulterated ecstasy.

Never in my life had I experienced this.

Freedom from thinking, freedom from worry, just being.

A hand settled on my chest. "Breathe, beautiful Sophia. Your tears and passion are a gift."

He released my wrists from the restraints. When I lifted my lashes as he pulled me up to sit, I realized I'd closed my eyes at some point during my orgasm.

A slight smirk touched his lips as he cupped my face. "Did you say something about one of us breaking?"

"That was incredible, so I will allow you to win that one."

"Most definitely a brat." He kissed me, first with slow passes, then deepening the embrace and driving up my need before pulling back. "I never found brats appealing until you."

"Don't get used to it. I'm one of a kind, Damon."

"I wouldn't dream of it." He reached to his side, grabbed a condom, and rolled it on.

My heart hammered into my chest as it registered in my addled brain that he was naked before me.

How had I not noticed he'd taken off his clothes? And holy fuck, it was as if a honed Adonis stood before me with a cock ready to tear me in half.

He pulled me forward, spreading my thighs apart. My arousal continued to hum from my orgasm a moment earlier, but an uncertainty prickled the back of my mind.

Should I say something?

Damon threaded his fingers into my hair as if sensing my worry and tilted my head back. "Have you changed your mind?"

My breathing grew unsteady as goosebumps

covered my skin. The crest of his thick hard erection nudged my swollen sex, igniting the need in my core.

"No. But there is something you should know." I set my palms on his shoulders.

He pushed in a little further, and I bit my lower lip, filling the stretch beyond those of my toys.

"And that is?"

I wrapped my legs around his hips before I gave him the answer. "I've never done this before."

A feral light entered his emerald gaze, and he grabbed my throat, bringing his face a hairsbreadth from mine.

"Never?"

The intensity of his question had a pang of uncertainty settling in the pit of my stomach.

Would he stop? Would he reject me?

He preferred women with experience. I'd known that from the beginning, and I was the furthest thing from it.

Whatever happened, I'd handle it. Just as I'd dealt with every other time, someone turned away from me.

I held his stare and answered, "Never."

"You have no idea what that means, Only

Sophia." He slid in some more and then took hold of my ass in his hands.

"What does it mean?"

"I own this pussy." He covered my lips with his and slammed in, making stars appear in the back of my eyes.

The feelings of fullness and heat of him inside were like nothing I'd experienced before, both painful and delicious.

He remained still, waiting until I relaxed, and then asked, "Are we good?"

"I've never felt so full."

"Only Sophia. I'm not even all the way in."

Oh, dear God. He was going to tear me in half.

Those thoughts only had moments to linger as he pulled out and thrust back in. This time I knew he was completely in. His pelvis touched mine, and there was no space between us.

The pulsing of his cock sent tremors throughout my core, and I couldn't help but squirm, needing him to move to give me the pleasure that awaited.

"So greedy," he hummed and then added, "As you command."

There was no missing the humor in his words as he started a slow rhythmic pace. Immediately sensations overwhelmed my senses, and the only thing I could focus on was the mesmerizing eyes of the man who held me captive.

My pussy flooded with desire, and my breast swelled and ached as they grazed his light dusting of hair on his chest with the movement of our bodies.

I wrapped my arms around his neck and held on, knowing I had no control over this. He rolled his hips in a precise way, causing my orgasm to come out of nowhere. It made my back bow, and I scored my nails over Damon's shoulders in ecstasy.

I'd barely come down when he said, "You have to give me at least two more before we're done."

I stared at him as if he'd lost his mind. A determination lit his eyes, and something clenched in my heart. This man was different. He held so much back, and I'd only gotten a small part of him tonight. Not even close to the real man who existed.

Deep inside him lay a darker essence that called to me. I wanted that part of him.

The thought evaporated from my head as Damon's thumb grazed my clit, and I all but bucked against his pounding cock.

"I changed my mind. It would be best if you gave me three more. Then we're done."

"You're going to kill me."

His face darkened for a moment.

"What did I say?"

Then a smirk touched the corners of his lips. "Death by orgasm. That's a club first."

CHAPTER SEVEN

Damon

WHAT THE FUCK have I done?
I dropped my head back onto the couch where I sat and gazed up at the intricately decorated ceiling of the playroom. I'd just spent the last three hours with Sophia. She slept peacefully against me, spent from play and sex. However, my mind warred with itself and the consequences of tonight.

I couldn't shake the sense that I'd fallen down a rabbit hole without comprehending when I'd reach the surface again.

I should have walked away the second she'd given me her name and I connected the family resemblance, but more so when I realized she was Lucian's baby sister.

Then again, I'd never felt this extreme a draw toward any woman before Sophia.

The desperate need to taste her, touch her, and ultimately fuck her won out.

Now by doing all three, she'd blown my mind, and I wanted more—more of her cries, more of her desires, more of her submission.

Exploring, she said. Not a submissive, she said.

How could someone like her not know what she was?

Her reaction to me in the bar alone conveyed her tendencies. Anyone who'd watched our interplay would agree.

Why hadn't I paid attention to the warning of that visceral pull we had to each other?

The intensity of it surpassed anything I'd experienced with anyone before her.

Guilt shot deep into my gut.

I'd driven Maria to her choice. I couldn't allow another to fall onto the same path.

One night only. That's how I'd prevent it. We'd go our separate ways after tonight.

Hell, I may not have to worry about the decision anyway. I expected at least a few scathing, if not graphically, incensed calls from Lucian about my upcoming demise for touching his baby sister.

I was one of the few people he couldn't intimidate. So technically, his threats were just him blowing off steam.

However, I'd crossed a line in our friendship

by touching Sophia.

Bro code and all that jazz.

There was no doubt that within a few seconds of Sophia and me moving in the direction of the playrooms, Ventana or another of the club members sent Lucian an update.

Would I have stayed away from her if Lucian ordered me to do it?

Fuck. I had no idea.

I lifted my head and stared down at Sophia's dozing form draped across my lap and tucked under a blanket; naked, relaxed, and sated.

She'd given me so much more than I expected tonight.

The wild child daughter of the Morellis, the one in all the tabloids who flaunted one high-profile relationship after another. She was a fucking liar.

I'd taken from her, loved every second of it, and wanted to defile her in so many more ways.

She'd blown every barrier I'd meticulously erected over the last year and a half into tiny pieces in the matter of one night.

She fucking made me want, she fucking made me crave, she fucking made me need.

Never had a woman cried such beautiful tears or begged so sweetly.

Her submission tasted better than the most decadent of aged cognacs.

There truly was nothing like watching her surprised gasps as she realized she enjoyed the bite of pain administered from a flogger. Or how she'd arched, anticipating the next strike but never knowing when it would come.

The desire to own her, possess her pumped through my veins.

The thought of taking her to my home and tying her to my bed or using her to recreate the photo she'd enjoyed outside this room had my cock growing rock hard.

Warning bells blared in the back of my mind, bringing me back to reality.

I couldn't get carried away. Once was enough. Never again.

She'd hooked me, but I refused to let it happen in return. I'd save her from me.

Sophia's lashes fluttered open, and her onyx eyes peered up at me with a tinge of sleep lingering.

This was the moment to do it, end it, cut it off, and make it so she'd never want to see me again.

Her gaze heated, and my need for her hummed in my blood. She parted her lips a fraction, but it gave me wicked thoughts of gagging her with my cock and watching beautiful tears fall from her eyes.

Then her expression changed to weariness and uncertainty.

I fucking couldn't do it. Not at this moment, with her so vulnerable and expecting a blow that would destroy her.

"Did you have a nice nap?" I brushed the hair from her forehead.

Tucking her feet under her, she pushed up to sit with one hand. The blanket slid down, exposing her perfect breasts and the faint red marks from the flogger.

My lust surged, and my dick stiffened into a thick hard rod, ready to fuck her raw.

"Yes," she responded as a blush crept along her lightly tanned skin and up her cheeks. "What happens now?"

This woman, who understood fashion and the use of her body to gain the right reactions, hadn't a clue how her shy awkwardness affected me.

I cupped her beautiful face, rubbing a thumb over her plump lower lip. "First, I need to know how you are doing."

She turned her face away as the flush on her skin deepened, and the deep innocence of Sophia

Morelli radiated out from her. The piece of her I refused to corrupt and break apart.

Tugging her chin back to face mine, I leaned toward her. "Why are you acting so shy now, Only Sophia? Haven't I touched every part of you tonight?"

"You can call me Sophia. You already know I'm a Morelli."

She'd quickly replaced her shyness with an edge of irritation when she said her last name, piquing my curiosity about which family member she clashed with the most.

Her father or mother.

Maybe both since she tended to scandalize the whole family based on what I knew about them.

Why had she let them believe the worst in her? And why the hell was she hanging out with all those assholes who would sell her story to the highest bidder in the first place?

The urge to protect her, keep her, shield her from the world nagged at me.

"Sophia, how are you feeling? Be honest."

"Sore. Nothing serious." She held my gaze. "I enjoyed it."

"I know." I smiled at her. "Are you still exploring, or can you admit your nature?"

A crease formed between her brows. "I'm not

submissive."

"Is that right?" I slid my palm down her throat, holding her firmly and giving her a light squeeze.

Immediately her pupils dilated, and her breaths grew unsteady. Her fingers wrapped around my forearms as she closed her eyes in blissful surrender. Goosebumps appeared on her skin, and she bit her lower lip.

"You were saying?"

Her lids snapped open. "You're a good-looking man. What we have is called attraction."

"We definitely have attraction in spades." I brushed my lips against hers. "I could grow attached to you, Sophia Morelli. You are so fucking addictive."

She circled her arms around my neck and climbed over my thighs to straddle my lap. However, a knock sounded on the door before she could situate herself.

Resisting the urge to clench my teeth, I glanced at the clock on the wall.

The three-hour mark. The maximum time limit for club members using private rooms.

I was part of a group of Doms who were exceptions to the rule. But not tonight. It looked as if Lucian wanted me away from his sister. I'd better get ready for a visit from the asshole.

"It looks as if our time in the room is over."

She released a sigh. "I knew it would come."

I offered her my hand, and she slid from my lap.

Over the next few minutes, we both dressed, preparing to leave. Watching Sophia set her façade back into place step-by-step fascinated me. It was as if every layer she added, from her makeup and clothes to her jewelry and shoes, added another level of armor.

Once she finished, the innocent Sophia I'd unwrapped had all but disappeared under the guise of the Sophia Morelli the world saw.

"Will I see you again?" she asked after I walked her out of the playroom and to the hallway near Lucian's private exit for the club.

This was the moment I had to do it. I couldn't wait any longer. Being a bastard to a woman wasn't in my nature. Yeah, I enjoyed all that came with kink but purposely hurting them. No. I wouldn't be like my father, who enjoyed it like a sport.

I'd made a vow never to become that bastard. It was better to be honest than to tell a lie.

Shit. I'd hurt her no matter what I'd said.

I shook my head. "No. We should never encounter each other again."

Hurt and confusion cascaded over her beautiful features. "I don't understand. You said you could grow attached to me."

"That's the issue. I'm not good for you, Sophia. I'm trying to be a gentleman. You don't want any part of who I am."

"Isn't that my decision?"

"No." A frown marred her face, but before she could argue, I continued, "What you experienced tonight isn't even the beginning of all I want to do to you. You saw the gentle side of me. That's not who I am the majority of the time."

Her eyes flared with desire. "What would you do if you weren't gentle?"

"I want to bind you, gag you, fuck you, destroy you, make you mine inside and out."

"I don't understand. Why is that bad?"

"Because in the end, I will break you. I am everything that is wrong for you. It would be best if you ran from me as far as possible. I am the worst thing that can happen to someone like you." I shook my head, gripping the back of my neck.

"I'm not afraid of you. I want to explore more of what we did tonight and go further."

Fuck. She just wasn't listening.

"You're too innocent and don't have any concept of how far I can go."

"You can show me."

"No. I want a submissive with experience who knows what I expect of her. When I come here, the last thing I want to do is train anyone."

Not sure whether my words or the determination on my face penetrated her thoughts, she nodded.

"Fine. I won't see you again."

✧ ✧ ✧

"Where are you?" Lucian demanded the second I answered my cell on Monday morning.

Turning my chair to look out at the streets below the high-rise window of my office, I responded with, "Working. Most people do that at the beginning of the week at nine AM. Don't Morellis work? Or wait, you're Lucian Morelli. So you do whatever the fuck you want."

"Funny, asshole. I'm coming up. We need to have a chat."

I stood and leaned an arm against the floor-to-ceiling windows. "By all means, let me rearrange my meetings for you."

"I'm sure you can fit me in for this discussion." He hung up, leaving me to shake my head.

I'd expected this conversation to come sooner. More along the lines of some time between one in the morning when I left Violent Delights on Saturday and Sunday afternoon. For him to have waited this long meant he had other things on his mind besides ordering me to stay away from his sister.

He'd have to get in line. I'd given myself plenty of warnings since I watched Sophia's voluptuous round ass disappear down the dimly lit corridor exiting the club.

Even now, I was half-hard thinking of her.

This spell she'd cast upon me made absolutely no sense, and the fact she had no clue that she'd done it added to her fucking appeal.

"Give me one good reason why I shouldn't kill you?" Lucian asked as he strode into my office and then shut the door behind him.

"For one, I'm in charge of designing four of your latest projects." Annoyance flared in Lucian's dark gaze, but he kept quiet as I continued, "And the decisions of two consenting adults are none of your business."

"She's my baby sister. Of course, she's my fucking business." He took the chair on the other side of my desk, continuing to stare daggers at me.

I remained standing just to fuck with him.

We were both assholes. However, in my office, I got to play the bigger one.

"Why did you give her access to your club if you weren't going to allow her to participate?"

A crease formed between Lucian's brows, and if I wasn't mistaken, the vein on his forehead began to pulse.

Yeah, annoying him for the hell of it was childish, but he fucked with my morning. I'd already made my decision about Sophia. His coming here seemed to have rubbed salt in the wound.

"Will you sit the fuck down?"

"No. Answer my question."

"It's safer for her to explore in my place than anywhere else." He followed my movements as I paced back and forth along the windows, his irritation growing by the second.

"She did exactly that. I kept her safe, and she had the chance to explore. What is your problem?"

I already knew the answer and just needed him to admit it.

"She's off-limits."

There it was.

"Why?" I moved to my desk, bracing my hands on it.

"You know fucking why?"

"So she's good enough for Ventana and the other Doms but not me?"

Lucian shifted forward. "I don't want Ventana touching her either."

"Bullshit. Just admit the truth. You don't want me touching her." I couldn't hide my anger.

"I won't have her wrapped up in you, and then you break her heart."

Clenching my jaw, I gritted out. "I didn't kill Maria."

He knew the truth. He'd been there when all of it happened. However, I'd always suspected Lucian believed, just like I had, that I'd driven Maria to her decision.

"This isn't about Maria."

"I call bullshit again." I stood, turning back to face the window.

"I saw the feed from the bar." Lucian's tone grew hard. "I don't like the way she reacted to you."

"Meaning she found me worth her time while she dismissed everyone else?"

Instead of responding to my question, he added, "I also noticed how you looked at her following your session. She got to you, and now, you want to keep her."

Facing him again, I said, "Never realized you enjoyed voyeurism, Morelli. You'd have heard me warn her away as she left the club if you paid attention. Nothing to worry your sadistic mind over. Nothing is going to happen between us again."

"Now I call bullshit. Whatever happened between the two of you in that room, it fucked with you. Sophia doesn't need any more trouble. I'm warning you, Pierce. Stay away from her. I'll take care of you in the most painful way possible if you don't heed my warning."

"Did you forget I don't scare easily? I'm one of the few people you can't intimidate." I smirked at the glaring Lucian. "But I hear what you're saying."

Objectively, I understood Lucian's point of view. One of his friends had slept with his sister and wanted to continue to do so. It crossed a line into uncomfortable territory. I'd broken bro code, but for some fucking reason, I couldn't muster a single ounce of guilt over it.

However, I'd stay away for her sake, not for Lucian's.

"Then we agree. You'll keep your hands off, my sister."

I thought for a moment. Sophia Morelli had

crawled under my skin, and I wanted to gorge on her moans, cries, and tears. If she came to me, could I resist her?

Not a fucking chance.

"I won't seek her out."

"I should put a bullet in your head right now."

I shrugged. "Doing that will only hurt your business in the long run."

Lucian stood, moving to the door. "I'm going to hold you to our agreement. Do not go after her. I know you want to."

"How do you know what I want?"

"Because you're an obsessive, possessive bastard that's found something he can't have."

"Since you look at one in the mirror every morning, you would know, wouldn't you?"

CHAPTER EIGHT

Sophia

"I STILL THINK we should hide her stomach with an empire waist. Do you realize how form-fitting that gown is?" my mother asked as I adjusted the train on my sister Eva's wedding gown. "Everyone will know she's six months pregnant."

From the moment Mom learned of Eva's pregnancy, her feelings about the situation ran the gamut of emotions. From happy because it meant Eva finally landed a man to horrified, scandalized that her favorite child had sex and then found herself knocked up before marriage.

When Eva suggested I design her wedding gown, Mom agreed without consulting me. The last thing she wanted was for any renowned designer to learn of her daughter's condition or have it leaked to the press. Mom's image and standing in society meant everything to her.

I would have said yes anyway. Creating a

custom gown for Eva meant an opportunity to showcase the skills I'd learned through my many years in the fashion industry. Somehow Mom always managed to steal my thunder.

Fuck it. I was still designing a kickass, sexy as fuck dress for my very pregnant and beautiful sister.

Glancing up at Eva, I rolled my eyes. "We're not hiding anything, Mom. Eva is happy to be pregnant."

"What about the pictures? One day your child will see them and learn when they were conceived." She shook her head and then pinched the bridge of her nose.

"Don't you think the fact the wedding happened a few months before the baby's birth would give it away?" Eva shot a glare over my shoulder. "My kid's going to know their mom and dad had sex before marriage."

"Eva," my mother exclaimed, getting to her feet with irritation written all over her face. "I'd expect a response like that from her, not you."

"Oh, Mom, haven't you figured out Finn Hughes corrupted Eva, and now she says all the wrong things? Just like me."

"Sophia, really. Sometimes, I don't know what to do with you."

I would have thought my mother's exasperation comical if I hadn't known she was one hundred percent serious. She honestly couldn't understand how I'd turned out the way I had.

I should want a rich and powerful man to give me security and children, someone who aligned with my social standing and place in society. And to attract those types of men, I needed to behave as if I were a proper lady with grace and decorum. I shouldn't attend wild parties, walk the runways of various fashion weeks around the world, or find articles about me published on gossip sites and pages.

"Let me handle this," Eva whispered, setting a hand on my arm, and then said. "Mom, do me a favor and review the menu you requested for the cocktail reception you're hosting with Dad next week. I want to ensure everything is up to your specifications before placing any orders with the vendors."

Leave it to my big sister to play interference, as always. But then again, no one could handle our parents the way she could. Where I took the blunt approach, she maneuvered in strategic finesse.

Technically, I possessed the same skills. However, I chose not to utilize them when it came to my family.

"Don't think I don't see through you, Eva Morelli." My mother's tone lightened, and she gave her a slight nod. "Since both of you are determined to ignore my advice, I'll let the two of you finish the fitting."

When she moved to the door, opened it, and paused, I waited to hear whatever last statement she had to make. Of course, Mom always had to get the last word.

"Sophia." Her green eyes locked with mine. "I know you think I'm old-fashioned. But I have my reasons. Sometimes you have to play by the rules given to you, not the ones you wish you had. You're still my child, and I want the best for you."

With her head held high, Mom left the room, and all I could do was stare at the now-closed door.

"I only want her to accept me."

Eva sighed. "The foundation of every Morelli kid's pain."

"I'm not what she thinks I am." Why the hell had I said that?

"None of us are." She rubbed her very round belly. "Would anyone have believed I'd find myself in this predicament?"

I smirked, "I only hoped you had some wild

side hidden in you. At least I know you aren't a blessed virgin in your thirties anymore."

"Oh, that was lost before I hit my twenties," Eva muttered as if a memory flashed before her eyes.

"Is that right?" I hummed. "Do tell me more while I tailor this gown into something that gives you the aura of a sexy fertility goddess on your wedding day."

The last thing I wanted was to put shadows in Eva's eyes when we were here in honor of something beautiful.

Eva pursed her lips and gave me a beaming smile. "Let's leave all ghosts in the past and keep our focus on the fertility goddess part. I do like the sound of that."

"One gorgeous deity coming up." I moved behind her to make a few tweaks to how the fabric lay across her lower back.

The design of the dress fit Eva's personality—elegant, classy, and timeless.

She'd never fit entirely into a daring modern look, but she'd push it a little bit just for the right effect.

I peeked at Eva, who still held her hand against her bump.

She held so many secrets. She rarely shared

any of hers with anyone but my brother Leo. They had a bond I envied.

The closest person I had was Lucian. We were the troublemakers of the family, the black sheep, as they say.

He knew things about me that I'd never tell anyone else in the family. Such as my interest in kink. But I couldn't divulge all my secrets to him. There were limits. He'd lose his shit if he knew some of the things I'd gotten into over the years.

Well, come to think about it, he'd either lock me away to keep me from going to jail or join me. One never knew with him.

Though for my current predicament, I needed advice only a big sister could give.

Since the moment I'd left the club a few days ago, a riot of uncertainty churned continuously inside me.

How could I want a man who'd warned me away with such passion, such dangerous intent, such command? It both scared and called to me.

Logic told me to listen and heed his order and my decision upon leaving the club. Except, this driving desire for Damon Pierce warred with everything I told myself.

I needed more of this fire he'd ignited inside me.

I'd never felt so free or cared for as I had in his arms. It made no sense.

I'd cried. I hadn't shed a single fucking tear under any circumstance since my late teens.

Why had I let my guard down so entirely with him? Was something wrong with me that I craved Damon's touch and the things he'd done to bring those tears to my eyes?

Taking a deep breath, I went for it. "Eva, can I ask you for some advice?"

"Of course." Eva's attention shifted to my face. "I knew something was wrong."

"Does my asking for advice mean something is wrong?"

"You let Mom get in a few of her barbs before cutting her off. Either you're getting sick, or something is wrong. And you never get sick."

I shrugged. "I was distracted."

"Obviously. Is it about someone you are seeing?"

Deciding there was no point in hedging, I responded with, "If you could call it that."

"Sophia, why do you date these guys that aren't worth your time?" Eva was the only person who could ask that without offending me.

She worried about me in her mother hen, big sister way but not in the holier-than-everyone, judgmental one. She never wanted me to walk away with a broken heart.

If she only knew, I'd never dated any of the men the press linked to me. The few men I'd gone out with were never in the limelight, and I kept those relationships quiet. And most of those ended once they realized things weren't going to pass into the territory of the bedroom.

All of a sudden, Eva's eyes grew wide. "Please tell me it's not that fashion designer who the tabloids said cheated on his model girlfriend. You aren't the other woman, are you?"

"Oh, for the love of God, Eva," I couldn't keep the exasperation out of my voice. "No. Give me some credit. And for the record, that's a publicity stunt."

Relief washed over her face. "I hoped it wasn't true. You're too smart for that."

"Then why did you ask?"

"I worry about you, and sometimes my imagination gets the best of me. Blame it on the pregnancy hormones."

I released a sigh. "You're forgiven."

"Who is he? A designer? Celebrity? Someone I've read about?"

"He's not in the fashion world. He's not in celebrity circles at all. He keeps a low profile."

"I need more details." Eva cocked her head to the side. "Let me take this thing off. We need to have a chat."

She stepped off the platform, undressed, and put on her day clothes. Then after I took the gown and draped it onto the sewing mannequin, we both took a seat on a nearby settee.

"Start talking," Eva ordered.

"Don't freak."

"You expect me not to worry after that kind of warning?" She gave me a side-eye.

"I met him at a club."

Her eyes narrowed. "I'm going to assume it wasn't a nightclub."

"I met him at Violent Delights."

I waited for a reaction, but she remained quiet. Though worry lit her eyes, and she wrung her hands together.

"I... I like him. He's different. When I'm with him, I feel things I've never felt with anyone else."

"Then what's the problem?"

"He told me he won't see me again."

"Why?"

"He said he's not good for me. He doesn't want to hurt me."

"Maybe you should listen to him."

"You don't understand. I've gone there so many times, and I have never wanted to do anything with anyone. Then I met him. How am I not supposed to feel that again?"

"I've never seen you react to anyone like this. Who is he?" Eva cocked her head to the side and studied me. "Is he someone I'd know?"

I hesitated for a second and then answered, "His name is Damon Pierce."

"You can't be serious." She grabbed my hand, clutching it in hers. "I can't believe Lucian allowed this."

"I'm an adult, Eva. I make my own decisions. I don't need Lucian's permission to sleep with someone."

"You don't understand. There are rumors about Pierce and his involvement in the death of his ex. I don't want you mixed up with someone like him."

The weight of resignation settled on my shoulders. It looked as if Damon Pierce and I weren't meant to be.

"He already warned me away. So you don't have to worry."

"By telling you upfront that he's dangerous, he saved you from all the heartache and pain other women endure before they learn the lessons of being with men who will only hurt them in the end."

The shadows entered Eva's eyes again.

"What if I never feel like I did the other night with anyone else again?"

"You will, I promise. And it may be ten times better."

✧ ✧ ✧

"TWICE IN ONE week. What a delightful surprise," I heard from behind me as I made my way through the employee hallways to the public playroom in Violent Delights.

Tate carried a case of drinking glasses in the same direction.

"How are you?" I asked, smiling at him.

"Excellent. Should I get your preferred cocktail ready?"

"No." I shook my head. "I may not stay long."

A grin tugged at his mouth. "Or do you plan for a repeat with a certain Mr. Pierce?"

My heartbeat accelerated upon hearing his name. He'd warned me away, and so had Eva. Nevertheless, the draw to him won out, and I couldn't stop myself from coming to the club.

"I'm only here to observe tonight."

He lifted a brow as if he believed otherwise. "We'll see."

"It's true. The other night was a one-time thing."

"Well, in that case, I have something special for you to observe."

"Okay, I'll bite. What is it you want me to see?"

He set his tray of glasses against the wall and gestured for me to follow him. "What do you know about Kinbaku, also known as Shibari?"

I couldn't help but smile. He was talking about the Japanese art of erotic rope bondage.

"Only what I've read about on the internet. I've never actually seen it live."

"Well, you're in luck tonight."

Tate guided me down the corridor leading into the playroom then pushed back a dark damask curtain, allowing me to enter the giant room.

Immediately, my attention went to the center stage where three couples were in various stages of bondage.

"Breathtaking. Don't you think?" Tate asked.

"Yes."

"The couples share complete trust. You can see it from the utterly blissful faces of the submissives, and their Dominants hold the same adoration for them in return."

"They are beautiful together."

"I see my work is done. Enjoy the show." Tate moved away, and all I could do was watch the stage as the group before me stirred something deep in my belly.

The first Dom had his sub tied in the shape of a flower and suspended from an apparatus connected to the ceiling. Her head hung back, and a smile touched her lips. The Dom rocked her in a slow back-and-forth motion as if lulling her to sleep.

Next to them, a Domme created an intricate pattern of knots with the hemp across the muscled chest of her kneeling sub. They spoke in hushed tones and kept constant eye contact. Love radiated out from the two of them and conveyed their committed relationship.

The last Dom had his sub hanging upside down, completely restricted from movement, in the shape of a turtle. The submissive deep-throated his Dom's cock between the push and pull of the harness.

My nipples pebbled, and an ache grew between my legs.

This was total submission, giving up complete

control. What would it be like to trust someone to that level?

The Dom relentlessly used his sub until he came down his throat. Then, he slowly bent down to his knees, and they stared into each other's eyes. The way he caressed his sub's face seemed so intimate. A private moment meant only for them, but I couldn't keep my eyes off the scene.

Was this the connection I sought so desperately?

A trickle of sweat slid down my spine.

"I told you not to come here?"

My head snapped up to stare into Damon's furious green irises.

It felt as if his whole body engulfed the space around me. He wore a fitted black shirt and dark denim jeans. His dark brown hair was unkempt and disheveled, not styled back as I'd seen him the last time. I preferred this look so much better. And he bore a dusting of a beard, making him appear dangerous and a bit intimidating.

The arousal that already coursed through my body from watching the couples bounded higher. This man drew me to him despite all the warnings—his and others.

I ached to press my thighs together and relieve the desire that stirred inside me from being near him.

"You told me to stay away from you. I am free to come here as I please."

Damon clenched his jaw. "Are you planning to play or observe?"

Irritation prickled the back of my neck. He had the nerve to ask me that question when he was inside the walls of this club, looking for an experienced submissive.

I was too innocent for him.

One night only, he'd said. I hadn't realized how much his words had truly hurt until now. Or maybe I had and just chose to ignore them.

"It isn't any of your business, is it?" I lifted a brow, then added, "Unless you've changed your mind about your warning from the other night."

"I'm not available to you."

Meaning no to me but yes to someone else.

"Thank you for the confirmation." I kept my face impassive, turned, and stepped toward the center of the lounge.

I refused to give him any reaction to the sting of his words. If I wasn't what he wanted, I'd find someone else.

I only intended to observe tonight but fuck him. I'd enjoy myself with another Dom. Why the hell not?

Why not start my sexual discovery adventure with two men in the same week?

Better late than never, Sophia.

"I did not dismiss you."

I paused and said, "You aren't my Dom. I don't need your permission. Have a good evening, Damon."

"We aren't done speaking."

Tilting my head to the side, I said, "Yes, we are. You warned me away. I'm listening. Tell me to stay defeats the purpose. Now, I will find someone who wants me."

"Sophia, the warning is for your own good."

Ignoring him, I made my way into the lounge.

My own good.

I had four brothers to tell me what was for my own good. The last thing I needed was another man to add to the list. I lived life on my terms, and no one stopped me. My parents had washed their hands of me long ago, and as far as I was concerned, Damon Pierce could do the same.

As I entered the main social space, I focused on Clark Ventana, who stood off to one side of the room near a high-top table. He held a glass of deep amber liquid in his hand as his sharp blue eyes scanned the crowd. The way he carried himself made him look as if he were a king surveying his subjects.

If only I could muster up even an ounce of attraction for him, then I wouldn't have to feel like a total loser. Unfortunately, the lady bits stayed completely dormant around the blond-haired, blue-eyed Norwegian god. My girl liked broody, green-eyed, brown-haired assholes.

With an internal sigh, I approached Clark, setting an elbow on the table.

"How are you tonight, Mr. Ventana?"

He lifted his tumbler to his lips, giving me a suspicious once over. "Good evening, Miss Morelli. I'm surprised to see you here."

"Why?"

"The question is, why aren't you in the company of Mr. Pierce?"

"He's not interested."

"Is that right?" He adjusted his stance, leaning toward me. "I highly doubt that. Were those his words?"

I lifted my chin. "His exact words don't matter. He made it very clear. It was a one-time-only thing."

"But you would have agreed to more, am I correct?" His penetrating gaze sent a shiver down my spine, making me feel as if he saw more than I cared to reveal.

"Does it matter?"

"Of course it does." He brought his face even closer to mine. "Are you here to observe or play, Sophia?"

I wanted to say neither. A glass of wine and my bed seemed the best option. I no longer jumped into stupid things out of hurt or rejection. When I decided on something reckless, there were reasons.

Instead of giving him the truth, I said, "I don't know."

"I believe you need to decide very fast."

"Why?" I'd barely asked the question when a hand wrapped around my waist, pulling me back against a firm chest.

Clark kept his attention on me. "That's why."

This whole time Clark had known Damon was coming up behind me. He let it happen. Then why hadn't he introduced us from the beginning? Probably for the same reason, Damon warned me away.

"Ventana, if you will excuse us. Sophia and I haven't finished our earlier conversation."

Clark set his hand over mine on the table, our gazes locking. "Sophia, would you like to speak with Mr. Pierce?"

"Stay out of this, Ventana." Damon's fingers

flexed on my stomach, and my heartbeat accelerated.

I guessed he wasn't used to anyone walking away from him. Welcome to the world of Sophia Morelli. I never stayed where I wasn't welcome. I never begged for anyone's scraps.

"The decision is hers, Pierce. She was already making the call as you approached."

Damon tensed, making me believe he thought Clark and I were discussing whether to play or not.

Why would he care even if we were? He told me he wasn't available for me.

"Is that right? Go ahead, Sophia. Make your decision. Are you staying with Ventana, or are you coming with me?"

This made no sense.

Clark tightened his hold over my hand. "She doesn't understand what you mean by discussion, Pierce."

"Yes, she does."

I turned my head, seeing the intent in Damon's gaze. He planned to punish me, make me beg, and then enjoy my tears.

I parted my lips, hoping to ease the unsteadiness of my breath.

I wanted everything I saw in his emerald

depths and more. This couldn't be normal, the way he'd captured my desire. I craved the things he promised in one look.

"Sophia, answer the question." The rough edge of Damon's voice sent a spasm shooting through my core.

"I'm going with you."

He nodded, and Clark released his hold on me.

"Pierce, I hope you understand what you're doing," Clark warned as Damon turned me.

Damon gave no response as he guided me toward the giant public playroom. Whatever he intended, it would be available for everyone to see.

My blood hummed with a mix of anxiety and excitement. It couldn't be any different than a fashion show. I'd strutted around in a bathing suit before. But doing anything intimate or sexual, I wasn't sure if it aroused or made me want to run.

I always had my safe word.

Marriage.

"It's too late."

Looking to my side, I asked, "For what?"

"Regrets."

"Regrets are for the weak. I'm not weak."

"I guess we'll find out soon enough." Damon

grabbed me by the throat, hauled me into a dark corner, and pushed me against a wall.

I barely had a moment to catch my breath before his mouth covered mine, demanding, devouring, consuming.

My body heated, and my blood hummed with needs I could not control.

A whimper escaped my lips as I held onto his shoulders and lost myself in him. His tongue thrust and rolled against mine in a seductive dance, sending every one of my nerves into hyper-alert.

I wanted more, so much more.

As if hearing my thoughts, his grip on my neck grew tighter, and he asked, "Is this what you desired? Is this what you came here to feel?"

"Yes." I arched up against him, the friction of his chest against my nipple a delicious torture. "I need it. Damon, please."

"I told you to fucking stay away from me." His hand roamed between my legs, cupping my pussy. "I told you what would happen if I got my hands on you again. But you had to come here."

"You rejected me," I gasped, grinding against him, desperate for him to touch me harder.

"And so you decided to offer yourself up to another Dom, thinking you were safe to explore with someone else because it was your brother's place?" He pushed the gusset of my underwear to the side and slid his fingers between my soaked folds. "So wet, so hot. Filthy girl, do you think I would allow anyone else's hands on you but mine?"

I couldn't think with his maddening strokes, meant to tease and torment. I dug my nails into his flesh, unable to do anything but hold onto him.

My skin burned with need, and the ache deep inside me wound tighter and tighter.

He pushed my thighs apart with his leg, pressed my back harder against the wall, and thrust two fingers into my sopping pussy, making me cry out in pleasure-filled pain.

"Oh, God. Damon."

"That's right. Let everyone hear you call my name."

The sensation of people watching us prickled along my skin and ignited a desperate, painful throbbing in my core.

"In fact, let them see." He turned me, not releasing his hold on my throat, only setting my back against his front.

Immediately, my eyes locked with a Dom passing by, and panic hit me. "I'm not ready for others to watch me."

"Too fucking bad. You wanted me. You get what I give you." Damon fucked me with his digits, rubbing that spot deep inside me meant to drive up my need.

The Dom smiled as interest and heat entered his eyes, but then his attention moved to Damon. That was when his expression cooled, and he continued on his way.

"Did you see what just happened?" Damon crooned into my ear. "I've ruined this place for you."

"I don't understand." I couldn't think with him working my pussy the way he was.

"From now on, no one will touch you in this club because they're scared of me. They know I'm territorial. They know Sophia Morelli's mouth, cunt, ass, everything is off-limits."

His crude words caused a lump to form in my chest. If he turned away from me, I'd have no place to go for a chance to explore any of this again.

"Why didn't you leave me with Clark if you didn't want me?" I couldn't hide the hurt or the need coursing through my body.

His thrusts grew harder, making me cry out and dig my nails into his forearms. "I never said I didn't want you. Wanting you and wanting you to be mine are two fucking different things."

A spasm shot through me, and I no longer cared about his anger at the situation. I had to come. I was desperate to come.

"More, Damon," I whimpered. "Please."

"More, is it?" His hold remained firm on my neck as his other hand pumped in and out, in and out, making my mind whirl. "I own this cunt. It has only ever known my cock, and it will remain that way. You will never pull what you just did with Clark again. Do you hear me?"

"I don't want anyone but you," I admitted.

His thumb circled my nub as his pistoning pushed me closer and closer to the precipice of climax. "You didn't answer me."

"Y-yes. I need to come. I'm almost there."

He stopped his movement, making me want to cry as my release all but fell away, leaving only the unquenched arousal churning inside me.

Damon dropped his forehead to the back of my head, his breath as unsteady as mine. "You don't agree for the sake of an orgasm, My Sophia."

I realized what he'd said.

My Sophia, not Only Sophia or plain Sophia.

"I told you what would happen if you didn't

stay away from me. I told you what I wanted from you. I made it very clear you weren't safe with me. Now you belong to me, whether I want you to be mine or not."

I tilted my head up to look into his piercing eyes. "If you don't want me, then let me go."

"I never said I didn't want you. Or weren't you listening?" The corner of his mouth turned up slightly. "As of now, you belong to no one else but me at this club. And the only way that changes is if I release you."

For the first time, I felt a sense of genuine fear of him, but at the same time, I wanted to know every dark thing he promised in his haunted green eyes.

"I'm not afraid of you."

"Liar."

Before I could respond, he sealed his lips over mine and resumed his ministrations between my legs. Within a few thrusts, my pussy ascended back to its previous quivering state, and I toppled over into ecstasy.

"That's it. Let me hear your moans. They all belong to me now."

I quivered and contracted around his fingers, soaking him and completely unabashed with the sounds of my pleasure.

"Damon. Just like that." I rocked against him, desperate to ride wave after wave of his wicked acts.

In the back of my mind, I knew I should have thought of the fact we were in the public playroom area, and the possibility of Lucian reviewing the club's feed was high. But the cascade of delicious oblivion coursing through me made it all but impossible to care.

He brought me up again, keeping me delirious until I couldn't think.

As I slowly came down, Damon fisted my hair and murmured, "Welcome back."

Unexpectedly, a sense of uncertainty filled me. But it dissipated when I saw the carnal desire still looming in his gaze.

"I take it that this is only the beginning of your plans for me."

"Excellent assessment, brat."

"I'm a brat now? I thought I was your Sophia."

He jerked my head back, sending exquisite prickles of sensation over my scalp. "They are one and the same. You're a brat, My Sophia."

"And do you think you can change me?"

"Oh, no. I told you. I'm going to bring every bit of that brat out of you kicking and screaming."

He brought my face an inch from his. "I'm going to bask in your tears, your cries, your punishments. Don't say I didn't warn you when you have regrets later."

"I've already told you. Regrets are for the weak. I'm not weak."

"That's true. To be a Morelli, you can't be weak. Just remember, I'm one of the few who isn't scared of any Morelli. That should tell you what I am."

I'd met very few men who weren't afraid of Lucian or his wrath. It looked as if Damon was one of them. I'd find out one day what sordid history tied them together.

"What are you?"

"The worst thing that ever happened to you, and now there is no escape for either of us. You belong to me now."

"I belong to no one but me."

"Still think you're exploring, do you?"

"I enjoy the way you make me feel." My breath grew unsteady, and my skin prickled. "It doesn't mean I'm submissive."

"Deny it all you want. The facts are the facts."

Using his hold on my hair, he pushed me down to my knees, and then with his other hand, he reached for the opening of his jeans.

My heartbeat pounded in my ears, knowing what he expected from me. Apprehension and need surged inside me. He pretty much manhandled me to the floor, and for some reason, I loved every fucking second of it.

What did that say about me? Nothing made sense since I met him, and at the same time, it felt as if this was what I'd waited for my whole life.

"I've never—" I broke off, as heat crept up my cheeks, reminding me he preferred experienced women.

As if sensing my uncertainty, he brought his precum-glistening cock a fraction from my lips and said, "Then it means I own your mouth too. Soon there won't be a part of you I haven't touched. Now open up and follow every instruction I give you."

Damon pushed into my mouth, giving me the first taste of his salty, sweet essence.

"That's it, breathe through your nose, and relax your throat. I want you to take all of me and let me see your beautiful tears."

He angled my head and worked himself first in shallow thrusts, then going deeper and more demanding. He allowed me no control. I held onto his jean-covered thighs and took what he gave me.

Damon thumbed the wetness from my cheeks. "You cry so perfectly."

Back and forth, he rocked me. His breath grew unsteady, and he clenched my hair with a brutal grip—fiery need shot throughout my body and wetness between my legs.

"You're going to take every drop I give you."

I stared up at him through wet lashes. His brutal beauty scared me in a way I couldn't understand.

Why him?

His attractiveness went beyond what I encountered daily. He possessed all the refinement of those born into the world of privilege but with the rough, jagged edges of a predator lying in wait prepared to devour you whole.

And what did it say about me that I wanted to be his prey?

Fuck, I was losing my mind.

A groan erupted from his lips, snapping me back from my thoughts and to his flushed face.

"Swallow, My Sophia. Let them see me fuck your perfect mouth."

He held me over him as jets of cum shot in spurts to the back of my throat. I swallowed and swallowed what felt like forever.

Slowly, Damon's grip loosened, and he pulled free of my lips, tucking himself back in his pants.

Through shallow, unsteady breaths, I tried to calm my body and resisted the urge to glance in the direction of the main playroom area.

I swayed slightly from the exhaustion, and immediately, Damon steadied me with a gentle touch to my shoulder.

Kneeling in front of me, Damon tilted my chin up. "Can you handle more, or are you too tired for further exploration?"

A smile tugged at his lips, which had me returning his grin.

"There's more?"

"Most definitely."

"Will it be out here?"

"No. When I fuck you, it will be in private."

I stared into his emerald eyes, unable to hide my confusion. "Then what did we just do?"

"I made it very clear to everyone, including you, that you're off-limits to anyone but me."

The intensity of his gaze sent a shiver down my spine. This man held the power to pull out emotions I refused to set free.

I couldn't let myself fall for him. I couldn't become another woman lost to a man who never truly wanted her.

I'd enjoy my time with him and then walk away.

I could do it. I could handle it.

CHAPTER NINE

Damon

"Why are you still giving me that look?" Sophia asked as she watched me in the reflection of the mirror across from us.

"You're doing it again," Sophia said the moment we walked through the doors of the private playroom.

Locking us inside, I turned to face her and asked, "What am I doing?"

"You're trying to decide whether or not to tell me to get lost."

I stared at her. The way she easily read me was unsettling as hell. Then again, she'd played me, or the better description for what happened would be that, like an idiot, I let her pull me into that stunt with Ventana.

It was evident to both Ventana and me she never wanted him from the moment she approached him. Logic told me he wouldn't have taken her up on the offer, not only for the sake of his relationship with Lucian but also because he'd seen the gutted expression on my face after Sophia had left the club the night we'd met.

However, the instant Sophia set her hand on Ventana's arm, jealousy and possessiveness overtook every rational thought in my mind.

I'd claimed her very publicly per club standards, which meant no one would touch her unless I agreed to share her or relinquished my rights to her.

I had no doubt Lucian learned of the incident within seconds of it occurring. I better ready myself for another impromptu meeting tomorrow morning.

"I should tell you this won't happen again."

"Is that what you want to tell me so you can return to your experienced submissives?" The edge in her question gave away her own jealousy about seeing me at the club.

I leaned back against the door and narrowed my gaze. "Don't think you have any possession over me, Sophia. I come and go as I please."

A cool, expressionless Morelli mask fell over her face. The one I'd seen Lucian don countless times, hiding everything from hurt to rage. However, she hadn't mastered it like her brother because the fire in her onyx eyes showed the sting of my words.

"Good to know where I stand." She stalked toward me. "Mind getting out of my way? I want to go home."

She waited without looking up at me. This was my chance to let her leave, end it, and not look back. The last thing she needed was to end up tangled in the web of troubles cocooning my life.

Before I realized I had spoken, I found myself saying, "I do mind. You wanted this. Now you get what I give you."

"The hell I will. You may have fucked my face in the corner of a public playroom, but I'm not someone you can toss aside when you need distance." Her lips trembled for the briefest of seconds before she reined in her emotions.

This woman was a walking contradiction. Confident, yet so unsure of herself at the same time. A fucking weakness for a person like me.

"What makes you think I had plans to toss you aside?" I shifted from my relaxed stance against the door and grabbed her waist.

Her breath hitched. "The way you're acting. You don't want me to be yours. I'm going to make it easy for you. I don't want to be yours."

Until her, I'd never liked mouthiness in a

submissive. I enjoyed my women compliant, those who wanted to serve and follow directions. Sophia had this way about her that edged the line between respect and disrespect, something I'd bet she learned to do based on her role in her family.

"It's too late for that." I walked her backward. "I claimed you. There is no going back now."

Before she could push out of my hold, we reached a couch, and I tugged her to straddle my lap as I sat.

"Let me go, Damon, or the wrath you'll face from Lucian will be unlike anything you've ever seen in your life."

I cupped her throat, drawing her face closer to mine. "Do I need to remind you that I have no fear of your brother?"

Anger radiated out from her flushed face.

She appeared so damn young more than the ten years that separated us. I wasn't ancient by any means at thirty-five, but her innocence made me feel as if I were decades older.

Maybe the vulnerability and purity she hid so deeply inside her drew me to her. I'd broken every decision I'd cemented over the last few years without much resistance. Now walking away wasn't an option.

"I don't understand you, Damon."

Instead of responding to her, I brought her head down against my shoulder, and we remained silent for a few minutes.

The pulse of her upset still lay heavy between us, but there was no helping it. She had no clue as to what she'd gotten herself into with me. Her life wouldn't be the same. People talked, and the rumors about me would reach the right or wrong ears.

"Answer this question for me," I broke the silence. "Why do you play the family troublemaker?"

She pushed up to stare at my face and shrugged. "I guess because that's what everyone expects of me."

"I've done my research on you."

A blush crept up her cheeks, but she held my gaze, trying hard to hide her embarrassment. "What did you learn about my dark past and naughty present?"

"You like to lie about who you are. You're a complete fraud."

A crease formed between her brows. "I don't lie. I am all of those things people say about me. I am the party girl, the Morelli wild child. I walk the runways of fashion shows and attend all the social events written about in all the tabloids.

Drugs, alcohol, sex. It's always around me."

She couldn't hide the bitterness in her words as she added the last part.

"And yet." I tugged her forward, grazing my teeth against her neck. "I'm the only man who's ever fucked you, put his mouth on your cunt, or made you come. Why?"

Her breath grew unsteady. "Because I'm selective."

"Selective, is it?" I massaged the toned muscles of her back. "It's so much more than that. You play into the image for a reason. How much of your life is fiction, and how much is true?"

"Why does it matter?" She pulled back, her dark eyes turning cold. "People believe what they want to believe. I stopped trying to fit in a long time ago. Now I say and do whatever the fuck I want."

"Do you really, or are you playing into the role given to you?"

"Why don't you answer the same question, Mr. Pierce? Then we will proceed with the discussion." She held my stare as if daring me to push further.

Here we were, back to the push and pull of only a moment earlier.

Then I saw it on her face, the knowledge. She

knew about the rumors, about what people said about me. Something clenched in my chest when at the same time I realized she didn't believe any of it. Not once had I spoken of it or given her any context, but she questioned the validity of the things said about me based on her experience.

I was all wrong for her, and she kept tugging at parts of me that wanted to keep her, possess her. And the fact she was one of my closest friend's sisters mattered not one tiny bit.

"Ask the question you actually want to be answered."

"Why do you let people believe you killed her?"

"Because I drove her to it."

She gasped in a sharp breath. "She took her own life?"

I nodded.

"Then you didn't kill her."

"Wrong." I kept my emotions locked away as I conveyed the next part. "My way with my submissives led them to give me every part of themselves, body, mind, and soul. And even though I care about them, I can never love them the same way they do me. And in the end, when she realized I could never offer her what she desired most, she refused to accept it."

"You believe her weakness is a reflection of yours?"

"Isn't it?"

"Were you honest with her?"

"Yes. I told her I could never offer her love in the traditional sense."

"Then you can't carry the guilt for her not accepting."

"It doesn't work that way. I didn't see the signs of her depression or her withdrawal. My responsibility was to take care of her and provide for her needs."

"You can't make yourself feel something you don't."

"I hope you remember this when I inevitably hurt you."

"You're warning me away based on a past experience. I'm not her. I don't want what she wanted. I like what I feel when I'm with you, but I'm not looking for forever. My safe word wouldn't be marriage if I was looking for the happily ever after and the white picket fence."

"Why did you come to the club in the first place? What drives this need to explore your submissive side?"

She furrowed her brows, and as she parted her lips to argue, I grasped her throat in a firm hold.

Immediately her pupils dilated, swallowing her irises as her breathing grew ragged.

"You're submissive, My Sophia. Not a top, not a switch, and not a Domme." I bit her lower lip hard enough to sting without drawing blood. "No matter how much you deny it, we both know the truth of it. Everyone in that playroom tonight knows the truth of it. You will admit it before our time is up. I guarantee it."

"Good luck with that objective," she murmured against my mouth. "No one can force me to do anything."

I grabbed her wrist, pinning them against the hollow of her back. "Submission isn't about force. It's about what you allow. You hold the power. If anyone takes without consent, they aren't worth your time."

"Is this the consensus for all the men in the club or just you? We know this isn't how things work outside of these walls."

The last part of her statement made me wonder if she was making a generalized observation or if she'd experienced something unsavory.

"I can only speak for myself, but it is the basis for power exchange."

"You play the broody, broken, novel hero very well, Mr. Pierce."

Her sentiment left an unsettled sensation in my gut. The last thing I wanted to do was go there. So I shifted her onto the sofa, pressing her front into the cushions and jerking her hips back.

"I'm no hero," I warned. "I'm exactly the opposite."

She blew hair from her face as she peered at me over her shoulder. "You don't scare me."

"Liar." I lifted her skirt and ripped her thong from her hips, making her wince as the tearing lace stung her delicate flesh.

"I don't need to lie when the truth works just as well."

Her constant defiance, mixed with the lust in her black eyes, prickled at every one of my instincts to tame her and make her admit her true nature.

The challenge, the back and forth between us, heated my blood in a way I'd never experienced. I could fucking grow addicted to it.

I pushed down my pants, letting my cock spring free.

"I'm the worst thing that happened to you, and you can't see it." Reaching to the side, I grabbed a condom, rolled it on, and aligned myself to her slick, swollen cunt.

"I'm a Morelli." She braced her hands against

the armrest of the couch. "I know how to spot the dangerous ones."

I slammed into her tight little pussy, causing her to cry out and propelling her forward. The way she squeezed me tight would have made a lesser man come on the spot. There was nothing like knowing I was the only man who's ever had the pleasures of this woman's body.

Fisting her hair in a brutal hold, I jerked her head back to look up at me. "You have no clue what I am."

"Maybe not, but I'll find out sooner or later."

"Yes, you will." I rolled my hips, making her gasp and clutch at my arm. "Don't say I didn't warn you."

"Warning heard." Then she added with a smirk, "And ignored."

"I punish brats, My Sophia."

Her pussy quivered around my cock, and she licked her lips. "Is that a promise?"

"You aren't going to like it." I ran my thumb over her mouth, then glided it down her abdomen and toward her clit, circling the tender bundle of nerves. "Only one of us is going to get to come."

"You wouldn't dare."

"Wouldn't I?" I adjusted her against the armrest, pumping into her with long, leisurely strokes and continuing to tease her clit. "One thing you will learn about me is that I don't say anything I don't mean."

"Then why bother arousing me?" she whimpered, her pleasure evident from the flush deepening her skin.

"Because it adds to your punishment." I fucked into her harder now, my need for her increasing. "You can only push me so far."

She pressed back against me, meeting each of my thrusts, the need to come driving her and making her forget it wouldn't happen.

"Please. I'm right there." She slid her hand between her legs, but I grabbed it and pressed her palm into the couch cushion.

"You don't come unless I give you permission." I caged her with my body and drove in and out of her like a madman. "You don't have it."

"Asshole." She shot a rage-filled death stare my way. "The hell I don't."

Except she'd lessened the impact of her ire with the tears streaming down her face making her desire, need, and anger so fucking beautiful.

I drove her to the verge of climax two more times just for the sadistic pleasure of seeing more of her tears.

"Damon, please. Let me come. I'll behave. I

promise."

"No, little liar," I responded as my balls drew up and my orgasm rushed through me.

"Bastard."

"For that, you'll have to wait to come until the next time we meet. You don't get to touch that pussy. Only I do." I pumped hard and fast, working the rest of my release into the oblivion of the perfection that was her body.

CHAPTER TEN

Sophia

"SOPHIA, YOUR GROUP goes on in twenty minutes."

I glanced away from the dressing mirror in front of me to nod to the production coordinator for one of the most anticipated events of New York Fashion Week. I'd spent the last hour and a half having my hair and makeup set to perfection before I walked the runway as a favor for my friend, Karina Mehta.

Karina was one of the most sought-after designers in the world, with her styles having taken the fashion world by storm over the last few years. She'd recently moved into high-end jewelry and decided I was the perfect model to showcase her new pieces with her couture collection.

"Remember to do that far-off dreamy thing you do with your face. I've specifically applied your makeup for that purpose."

I resisted the urge to roll my eyes at the world-famous makeup artist Natalia Carla, who currently studied my face from various angles.

"I know. I know. The show is all about seduction. Longing, need, yada, yada, yada."

"If all else fails, pretend you're dreaming about an orgasm from your new lover."

"Have I met this new lover?" I asked, lifting a brow. "Tell me about him. Is he someone in the industry? I do enjoy hearing the latest news about myself."

The last thing I'd do was share my private life with anyone, especially a gossip like Natalia.

"That's too bad. I'd hoped you'd shed the sexual frustration that surrounds you all the time."

A few models near me laughed, hearing the nonsense between Natalia and me.

"A woman only needs her hands or a toy to take care of that problem."

Damon's words flashed in my mind. *"You'll have to wait to come until the next time we meet."*

As if he would have let me come if I hadn't called him a bastard. And how dare he order me not to make myself get off.

As if he owned me.

And why the fuck had I listened? I never listened to anyone.

This is what I got for waiting until I turned

twenty-five to have sex. The first guy I slept with fucked all the brains and logic out of my head.

"True. I'll have to remember the name of whatever that toy everyone keeps raving about. It will help you loosen up. You seem extra irritable and controlled today. You're acting—" Natalia paused, tapping the blusher brush handle to her chin. "More...what's the word I'm looking for?"

Someone from behind her shouted. "Sexually frustrated than usual."

If they only knew how true it was.

"I hate all of you, I swear." I shook my head and joined in the amusement everyone was having at my expense. "Did you all forget I'm a Morelli? I am stoic and grumpy by nature."

"No darling, you're the dance on tables, wild child. You don't fit the mold." Natalia turned my chair. "Go put on that sheer curtain worth fifty thousand dollars that Karina designed and the millions in gems requiring its own security team. You're on in less than five minutes."

✧ ✧ ✧

"I KNEW THAT one would look perfect on you," Karina stated as I took my position with the rest of the models.

I wanted to kick myself for not making the

original fitting.

What Natalia meant by sheer was transparent. This dress, if one could call it that, covered nothing. Outside of the jewelry, glitter nipple covers, and the stone-encrusted thong covering my crotch, there was barely anything left to the imagination.

I gave Karina a tight smile, not knowing what else to do.

I'd better prepare myself for the fallout. I could hear it now. It would start with lectures about embarrassing the family right before Eva's wedding and go on to business dealing and social standing.

Always the fucking social standing.

"Your body was meant to wear authentic jewels."

I stared at her, cocking my head to the side. "Are you saying everything I have on, including my underwear, is authentic sapphires?"

"And diamonds."

Diamond nipple covers? Was this woman insane?

That's when I noticed the security team, whose attention focused solely on me.

I gaped at Karina as if she'd lost her mind. "You could have warned me."

"You would have said no if I had." She pursed her lips. "Tell me I'm wrong."

"I'm here as a favor, and you have me naked out there."

She shrugged. "You're already the troublemaker in the family. What's one more thing to add to the pile? Besides, you're only twenty-five with a killer body like that once. Rock it while you can and tell everyone else to fuck themselves."

"Easy for you to say. You're an only child." I frowned. "I'm never doing you a favor again."

Karina adjusted the draping of the fabric on my shoulder. "You say that every time. I swear, your skin tone and curves are perfect to showcase millions in jewels. I can guarantee that by the time you step off the runway, someone will have purchased all the pieces just because you wore them."

Yep, that was all my mother would want to hear. Some random guy bought diamonds and sapphires since I wore them as underwear.

"You are why I ended up in trouble with my family the last time I walked a runway. Why do I keep doing this to myself?" I glared at Karina.

"Because I'm irresistible." She batted her lashes at me. "I'll make it up to you. I promise. Now go do that thing you do with your face that makes everyone believe you're thinking of sex."

"You are testing our friendship, Mehta," I muttered over my shoulder as I stepped into position behind the model, about to take her spot to walk the stage.

The music changed to a sultry hip-hop beat, and the lights dimmed as the show producer cued me to take my place.

Think of sex. Well, until a little over a week ago, I'd never had sex. So what was the face I gave while walking the runway?

Umm. The hell. I'd wing it as I usually did.

The spotlight illuminated my body, and gasps emanated from the audience. That was the exact reaction Karina wanted.

Bitch knew how to make an impression.

"Go," I heard the producer order, and I moved.

I licked my lips, knowing that seemed to work, and then tossed back the hair on my shoulder, giving a coy smile to those seated to my right in the front row. I swept my gaze over the crowd and concentrated on swaying my hips to convey seduction while keeping in tempo with the music.

Suddenly, my breath caught as my gaze landed on deep emerald green ones. Lust and untamed desire stared at me, making my body react. Heat sizzled over my skin, and a desperate ache throbbed deep in my core.

It took all my strength to control my exhalations and keep my pace from faltering.

Why was Damon here?

Wasn't this the type of event he preferred to avoid at all costs? One couldn't disappear here. The point of a show was to see and be seen.

Reaching the end of the runway, I paused, pivoting my body. I waited a few seconds to allow the photographers to take their pictures.

Damon continued to hold me captive with his penetrating lure. The arousal I'd tried so hard to ignore for the last few days rushed forward, all but consuming me, tingeing my skin with sweat and need.

He'd denied me—the bastard.

The surge of annoyance brought back some semblance of sanity. Before I turned, I narrowed my eyes at Damon, and he smirked in response.

Asshole.

Turning, I returned to the staging area.

✧ ✧ ✧

AN HOUR AFTER the end of the fashion show and the publicity Q&A session, I stepped into the ladies' lounge set up for the models. Of course, it was more of a glorified bathroom, but whatever.

The second Karina gave me the all-clear, I handed over the jeweled undies and slipped on a pair of comfortable linen pants and a hoodie.

I cringed, thinking of the shit I'd hear from Mom or, God help me, Dad the moment they learned of what I'd worn for the show.

Karina owed me for spending the day naked. And she could afford it since some dumbass had bought the whole ensemble I'd worn before I'd taken two steps down the runway.

After taking care of business and washing my hands, I studied my face in the mirror above the sink.

That was when I heard the distinct sound of a whimper, and the hairs on my arms prickled. A flood of memories tried to push to the surface, but I wrestled them back.

Shifting my gaze from my reflection, I studied the stalls and saw a person crouched in the corner of one in the far back. Whoever it was, they couldn't stop shaking.

Immediately, rage consumed me as I remembered being a girl in a very similar position, at a different fashion show, in a different bathroom, not so long ago.

At the door, I said gently, "Hey, It's Sophia Morelli."

"Please don't let anyone in here." Her tears tore at my heart. "I don't want anyone to see me like this."

"Okay, let me lock the door."

Rushing to the main door of the lounge, I locked it and returned to the girl.

"No one can get in. It's safe to come out."

She unlatched the stall, and I found Alice, one of the younger models chosen to run the catwalk during fashion week. She was maybe seventeen or eighteen at most.

"I'm scared he'll come back."

My stomach clenched hearing her say those words. "Who will come back?"

"I can't tell you." She shook her head. "He said if I breathe a word of it to anyone, he'll make sure I won't work again."

For a split second, I felt a double vision come over me as if I were reliving my past.

"What did he do?"

"He… He…came in here while I was getting ready to leave." She looked away from me. "He wouldn't let me leave. He touched me. I think he would have done more if I hadn't bitten him."

That's when I noticed the bruise on her cheek.

I'd had something similar and lied to Leo when he demanded to know who hit me. I'd given him some bullshit story about getting elbowed at a club, not the truth that a fashion designer smacked me after I'd kneed him in the balls.

Sliding onto the floor next to her, I wrapped my arms around Alice and gathered her to me. "You protected yourself. You're strong."

"I don't feel strong."

"You are. Believe me, you are." I held her tight. "Tell me who it was. I can help."

"He's powerful. He has connections and lots of money. No one can help."

"I can. I'm a Morelli."

I wasn't that weak girl shattered by an adult world. I had my ways now.

"He'll know it was me who told you."

"I'll make sure you stay safe. Give me the name, Alice."

She remained quiet for a few moments and then said, "Keith Randolph."

Everything inside me froze upon hearing that name.

Keith Gilbertson Randolph. One of the three heirs to the Randolph mining family and a famous fashion designer. He believed his pedigree and money allowed him to do anything he wanted. And I guessed it had.

I never hated anyone as much as him. I wanted to erase his existence from the earth.

"I promise you now. He will pay."

"What are you going to do?"

"Let me worry about that. Right now, I need to make sure you are okay. I'll take you home and get you comfortable."

Alice nodded and closed her tear-stained eyes, hiccupping a few times, before wrapping her arms around me and releasing a fresh wave of sobs.

The more Alice cried, the more my anger churned in my belly. I had plans for that fucker.

I wouldn't call my brothers and make it easy.

I knew with one word from me, they'd take care of him. They'd make it hurt so much. They'd destroy him piece by microscopic piece. And I know for a fact Lucian would get a kick out of letting me watch him do it.

Maybe I should have told my brothers about what happened to me.

No, that would have been a bad idea. Even the thought of what they would've done scared me. My brothers were protective on a good day. If I'd told them Keith Randolph assaulted me, they wouldn't have just killed Keith. They'd have annihilated his name from existence.

I couldn't risk Keith's old money ties to bring anything down on the heads of anyone I loved. I'd hold my secrets until the day I died.

Oh, I couldn't wait to avenge Alice. That fucker wasn't going to know what hit him.

CHAPTER ELEVEN

Damon

WHERE THE HELL had she gone?

I maneuver around the swarms of celebrities and models mixed among what I assumed were fashion designers in search of Sophia.

I hated these types of events and avoided them, if possible. I only accepted the invitation to the fashion show because I'd heard Sophia was the featured model walking the runway.

Seeing her in her natural element was too tempting to resist.

And the inconvenience of rubbing elbows with pain in the ass A-listers was something I could manage for a day.

Who was I kidding? I dealt with even bigger assholes. Like Lucian, he wouldn't think twice about putting a hit out on me for engaging in unsavory actions with his baby sister in the middle of his club.

Instead of the confrontation I'd expected with Lucian. He'd sent a note via a carrier saying.

Break her heart, and I break you.

Which meant I needed to stay away from Sophia outside of the club.

Lucian saw the writing on the walls as well as I could. Inevitably, I'd hurt her, change her, and live up to the fact I was the worst thing that had happened to her.

Why had I come to a damn fashion show to see her? And what the fuck possessed me to buy the jewels she'd worn. A sapphire and diamond G-string.

I'd lost my ever-loving mind.

Who the fuck was I?

She kept breaking every barrier I attempted to erect. I wanted her. I craved her.

The drive to see her, touch her pulled at me. And the thought of anyone owning anything that had touched her body in such an intimate way made me want to smash their face in.

I'd watched how she'd captivated the audience the very second the spotlight focused on her. She epitomized sex and sin walking down the catwalk.

The primal urge to let every fucker lusting after her know she belonged to me had coursed through me. I'd never felt anything like it, not with Maria or anyone.

Then when she found me in the crowd, rage settled only to be replaced with the urge to fuck her, rut until I'd quenched every bit of my desire.

Thank fuck she'd turned away, or I may have caused an incident, then Lucian would have definitely put a hit on me.

I ran a hand through my hair and pushed past a set of divider curtains into a design studio setup. Bolts of fabric lay in stacks on tables, and sewing stations lined various spots along the walls. Mannequin forms sat in rows of fours in the center of the space with half-made garments draped across them.

A few people worked to put away material around sewing machines while others leaned over tables, folding fabrics, and placing them in bins. At a set of sofas sat a group of male and female models who seemed to be having an aftershow gathering.

A woman with bright blue hair looked up from near a sewing machine, and asked, "Husband, boyfriend, or investor?"

"What makes you think I'm any of the above?"

"First, with that custom suit, I doubt you wear anything off a runway. Second, if you can drop more than fifteen grand on a suit, you aren't some assistant working behind the scenes." Now she smirked. "And third, only husbands, boyfriends, and investors walk back here as if they have a right to look for whomever they damn well please."

"Interesting assessment. I'm not a husband, a boyfriend, or an investor."

She cocked her head to the side, doubting my response. "Who are you looking for?"

"Morelli."

A laugh broke out from the sofa section, followed by a series of rapid-fire comments among themselves.

"Natalia was right all along."

"That girl lied right to our faces."

"No, she didn't lie. She said she was single. She could just be banging him."

"I never pegged her to go for the intense, broody type," another model hummed.

"This one looks like he'd choke you if you got in his way."

They all laughed again, making me narrow my gaze. None of them were even trying to pretend they weren't discussing me.

This world Sophia occupied made no damn sense to me.

And why was I so irritated that she let this Natalia believe she was single when I'd only seconds ago confirmed her status?

The designer spoke, snapping me out of my thoughts, "I believe Sophia is in the sample room."

"And where is that?" I eyed her, having no clue what the hell one did in a sample room or where I'd find it.

"Around the corner down that hallway." She pointed to her right.

With long strides, I took the corridor. I reached the area filled with racks of clothes, shoes, purses, and every accessory imaginable. Everything sat in strategically placed sections based on color and style.

I heard her voice before I saw her. She leaned against a wall with a cell phone tucked against her neck. She wore an ivory jumpsuit, more casual than anything I'd ever seen on her. This was an outfit I'd expect her to sleep in or just lounge about in at home.

Her clothes starkly contrasted the runway makeup still adorning her face, giving her a hue of perfection that added to her Morelli beauty. However, if someone looked deeper, they'd see the shadows of exhaustion touching the corners of her eyes and the heavy set of her shoulders.

There it was, the unguarded vulnerability she rarely allowed anyone to witness. Gone was the façade, the armor protecting herself from the world.

Whoever she spoke to and whatever pain she felt at this moment gave me the urge to protect her, keep her, shelter her. I wanted her locked in my home, away from the world.

Getting too carried away with this possessiveness would only lead to trouble. I'd hurt her, destroy her with my needs and obsession, and when I couldn't give her what she desired, it would break her. I couldn't let what happened to Maria repeat with Sophia.

But everything inside me said it was already too fucking late.

I moved in closer to her.

"I want you to get tucked into bed and then sleep as long as you need."

She closed her eyes, dropping her head back against the wall.

"No, you don't need to worry about anything. You have security. Yes, I promise, I don't need them," she paused. "I have a backup team. My brothers keep me covered."

Sensing my presence, she opened her lids and

focused on me. Her barriers slid back up, and the cool mask of control settled into place. Well, except for the spark of attraction that flushed her cheeks.

"I'll check on you later tonight." She ended her call, setting the phone on a shelf near her. "Who allowed you back here?"

Slowly, I stalked in her direction. "No one allows me to do anything. I just do."

"Let me ask you a different question." She shifted her body, standing up straight and setting a hand on her hip. "Why are you here?"

"Isn't it obvious?"

"This is hardly your type of scene."

"And what is my type of scene, Miss Morelli?"

She held her ground as I approached. "Not a fashion show, during fashion week in New York City with half-naked models."

"It is when my submissive is the half-naked model." I gripped her throat and pressed her against the wall. "Didn't I tell you this body belongs to me?"

"When did this move outside of the club?" Her breath came out in short, heavy pants as she clutched my shirt with both of her hands. "You don't have any say in what happens in the real world."

"I have all the say when what's mine is on display for everyone to see."

"I'm only yours in the club, not here."

I traced a finger over the dark shadow appearing under her eyes. "You're exhausted. You need to take care of yourself."

"I'm a grown woman. I don't take orders from you."

"If that was true, what do you call what happened the other night?"

"Correction. I don't take orders from you outside of the club."

"I won't have you getting sick." I leaned forward. "You need to get some sleep."

She rolled her eyes. "This isn't my first fashion week. I'm a pro at this."

"You will take care of what belongs to me, Sophia."

A crease formed between her brows, and hardness shifted in the set of her jaw. She tried to push me back, but my body mass made it too hard to budge me.

"I don't belong to you."

"Want me to prove it?"

"Go right ahead." She lifted her chin.

Instead of retorting with words, I took her mouth, making her gasp and moan. Then, before she could deepen it, I nipped her lower lip hard enough to sting and pulled back.

Breathing heavy, she stared at me with undisguised hunger.

Fucking gorgeous.

I turned her and then walked her in the direction of a floor-to-ceiling mirror. Our eyes connected in the reflection, and her lips parted a fraction. I stood nearly a foot taller than her, and my wide frame engulfed hers in shadow.

Sliding my palm across her abdomen, I pulled her back to my aroused front. With my other hand, I took the zipper between her breasts and tugged it down.

"What are you doing?" She stopped the momentum of my fingers.

"Meeting your challenge." Capturing her wrist, I brought it to her side and continued to expose her cleavage and her taut stomach. "You only need to answer one question, and it will reveal whether you belong to me or not."

I cupped her breast, pinching her nipple, making it hurt, just to the point where she gasped and bit her lip to keep her cry from alerting others.

"Wha—what is your question?"

"Have you made yourself come since I denied

you?"

Her half-hooded gaze connected with mine in the mirror. "That is none of your business. We aren't in the club or in a scene. You have no control over me here."

"Such a liar." I tsk'd and squeezed tighter on her straining bud, eliciting a whimper from her lips. "Are you afraid to admit what I already know?"

"You don't know anything. I make my own decisions. And if you conducted the research you said you did, you'd have learned I do the opposite of what people order me to do."

I whirled her around, caging her against the mirrored wall.

Grasping her fingers, I pressed them against her fabric-covered clit, drawing circles around the sensitive bundle of nerves. "Then why haven't you used these to fuck your sweet cunt to orgasm? Why haven't you relieved yourself of the arousal I saw blatantly staring at me while you walked the runway today?"

"You don't know anything about what you saw." She dropped her head back and closed her eyes, completely lost to the sensations growing deep in her pussy.

"Do you want to come, Sophia?"

Her breathing grew ragged, and a tinge of sweat broke out on her brow as I used her hand to stoke her need higher and higher.

"Damon, please. I'm there. I'm almost there."

"Answer my question. Did you make yourself come? Or did you wait?"

"I'm not weak. I make my own decisions."

Pushing her fingers away, I took over, rubbing, teasing, driving her to the point of going over. "That's not an answer."

"Don't make me say it."

"You don't get to come unless you do."

She writhed, pressing her pelvis against my hand, urging me to let her fall over the cliff. A tear spilled from the side of one eye, and I leaned forward, licking it away.

"I hate you for making me cry."

"I love your every tear. Now answer the question."

She shook her head. "N-no. I waited. I fucking don't know why, but I waited."

"Good girl. Was that so hard to admit?"

Covering her mouth with mine, I sent her into the oblivion of release. Her nails scored my forearms, and muted moans escaped her lips. She tasted of cinnamon candy and her own natural sexy essence.

I ached to fuck her, bend her over the chaise in the corner from us, and drive into her, destroy that sweet tight cunt of hers. But this wasn't the time or place. I'd get my chance soon, and then I planned to gorge until I satisfied every one of my depraved cravings.

A better man would preserve some of her innocence, stop everything now, and keep this dynamic exclusively in the club.

Fuck. She was such a delicious temptation.

And I knew I wasn't even a good man, much less a better one.

She broke our kiss and looked up at me as if reading my thoughts. "I'm not weak or fragile, Damon."

"No, you aren't. However, I will test how strong you truly are."

"When did I agree to anything outside of the club?"

"What happened right now would say otherwise."

"I won't let you control me. I've had enough people telling me what to do and pushing me around my whole life. If the fear of my father's wrath hasn't forced me to fall in line, don't think you can sway me to do anything I don't want to do."

I knew all about Bryant Morelli's temper and how he delved out discipline toward his wife and children. He shared more similarities to my own father than I cared to think about. The only difference was mine no longer walked the earth, having died a few months before my graduation from college.

His death had freed my siblings and me from a raging alcoholic father, the trap of our family business, and the legacy of carrying on the Pierce name. The day we sold Pierce Holdings was one of the best damn days of my life. A fuck you to the man who believed that a fist was the best way to keep everyone in line, his social standing trumped anything, including his wife's cancer, and that the next deal was more important than his two sons and daughter.

"The very first night we met, I told you the submissive holds the true power."

"I'm no—"

Cutting her off, I said, "With me, you are. We've established this. Accept it."

"I won't become my mother."

"Is that what you fear? Becoming your mother? There is a huge difference in the dynamics between your parents and us. You want a firm hand to give you the freedom you only pretend to have with your wild antics."

"It's better than being a conformist like my sisters Eva and Daphne. This way, my parents have written me off for the most part and leave me alone."

"And it leaves you the loneliest person in the middle of the most exclusive party in town."

Her inquisitive stare blazed up at me. "Why do you care so much?"

"What makes you think I care?"

"You've obviously analyzed me in great detail." She shook her head. "And you've gone from telling me to run away from you as fast as possible to claiming me as your sub. Now you're here with this possessive you-belong-to-me shit."

"That makes you deduce that I care?"

"Evade answering all you want. I know you care." She pushed me back, moved past me, and tugged the zipper of her jumpsuit up. "Do you think I don't see it?"

This conversation needed to stop right now.

She felt something for me. I saw it growing from that first night. With Maria, I'd ignored it. I refused to do it with Sophia.

"You ignored my first warning, but don't this one. You don't want me to care for you. And you most definitely don't want me to love you."

She adjusted her stance and set a hand on her hip as if I'd thrown down a dare, and I fucking knew the brat wasn't going to listen.

"Why is that?"

"Because I'll want to not only claim you, I'll want to possess you. No, I will possess you. I will own you. And that freedom you crave so much will disappear."

"It's good I don't have to worry about you loving me. Since you told me, it's an emotion you can't feel."

"Then I guess we understand each other."

"I think it's you who doesn't understand. This." She gestured between us. "Stays at the club. Don't come to me like this again. I won't let you blur the lines because you can't help yourself. I'm Sophia Morelli. I'm worth so much fucking more than a man's scraps and a bag of guilt."

CHAPTER TWELVE
Sophia

"LIZZY. WHAT ARE you doing here?" I ask as I step into my living room a little before nine in the evening, the night after the runway show.

The youngest of the Morelli children never dropped in anywhere without an ulterior motive. And of course, the evening I planned to take care of some pressing business, she decided to make her inconvenient visit.

Her scrutinizing gaze took me in, inspecting me from head to toe. Naturally, I gave her the same assessment. She looked overall healthy, except for a few shadows under her eyes, which told me she needed some sleep.

I knew the exhaustion wasn't from the wild party college scene. Those actions were more or less me. Lizzy was more of an old soul in the body of someone who had just turned twenty. I also saw a loneliness in her that I wished never existed, which I saw reflected in my own eyes when I looked in the mirror each morning.

What I wouldn't give to shelter her from being a Morelli offspring.

"I was thinking about you all day and decided to come see how things were going in your life."

Moving into my living room, I sat on the couch across from Lizzy, tucking a foot under my knees. "I'm not buying it. What do you want?"

"Can't a girl visit her big sister?"

"Ummm." I tapped a finger on my lower lip. "No. Not you. You're the text first, then call, then visit because you need something type. What is it that's bothering you? Spit it out."

She leaned forward and gave me a death stare. "I want to know what you're about to do?"

"Excuse me?"

"You heard me. I felt it when I woke up this morning. You're up to something."

Maybe she had a touch of clairvoyance.

"Well, I had plans tonight to go out, but other than that, nothing special."

"Then you won't mind if I tag along?"

"It's not your kind of scene."

A scowl formed on her face. "How do you know? I'm not as innocent and naïve as you think I am."

"It isn't like that. What I intend to do tonight isn't exactly—"

Before I could finish, she jumped in, "Are you going to do something illegal?"

For a second, I thought about lying to her, and then I decided to say, "Possibly."

"I knew it. My gut said you were up to something nefarious."

I lifted a brow at her use of the word "nefarious."

"That's why you came over? Your gut told you to do it?"

"Someone in the family has to make sure you don't get into trouble."

"Too late for that. I'm a lost cause, remember?"

She folded her arms. "I'm coming with you. Take it or leave it."

The stubborn set of her jaw and the way she tried to look all stern had me biting my lips to keep from laughing. Lizzy possessed not a single intimidating bone in her body.

"I don't want you involved in this."

"I don't care what you're doing. You're not going alone."

"No."

"Yes."

"No."

"I'm either your sidekick in this adventure, or I'm ratting you out to Lucian. Take it or leave it."

I gaped at her.

"Blackmailing your own sister, I see. So I guess you aren't the nice Morelli after all."

"Maybe I was always like this, but since I'm the youngest, no one noticed."

"What made you decide to assert your skills on me?"

"I knew you'd say no, and the only person you listen to is Lucian. So I thought, why not threaten you with him."

"What about our other brothers? Didn't think to use them?"

"No. Lucian is the ace in the hole when it comes to you. With both of you being the outsiders in the family and all."

I signed. "That we are."

"I didn't mean it like that." She grew quiet, released a deep breath, and then continued. "College made me realize a lot of things about our family."

"Like?"

"Mom and Dad don't even know me. They have an idea about who I am, but how do they know any of it is true? I'm the youngest, the baby.

I'm just there, so I follow along. That got me thinking about you. Everyone makes assumptions about you, but how much is fact, and how much is fiction?"

Her words felt like a fist to the gut.

I'd waited years for one person in the family to acknowledge just maybe the things said about me were lies. And it turned out to be the youngest of us who questioned everything.

"I'd say twenty percent fact and eighty percent fiction."

"In other words, you push Mom and Dad's buttons as retaliation."

"Not anymore. Maybe when I was your age, now I don't care. No one cares what I do anymore as long as I don't embarrass the family. Image is everything to Bryant and Sarah Morelli."

"I care. That's why I'm going with you when you do whatever you plan to do tonight."

"Tonight's activities go in the twenty percent category."

"I figured."

"Okay, then. Get up. You need to get changed. Don't bitch if things go sideways, and I scar you for life."

✧ ✧ ✧

"What are we doing here?" Lizzy asked me for the tenth time after exiting the subway station near Keith Randolph's Central Park apartment building.

The last thing I planned to do was give her details of my plan. Having her come with me was terrible enough. The train ride over had gotten me thinking Lizzy needed no part of my plans, but it was too late.

I only hoped she kept it together. At least convincing her to wear a disguise hadn't been hard. Colored contacts, high-end wigs, the right clothes, and the look of a call girl to the elite unfolded.

Only someone who expected or knew we were in the area would have recognized us.

I turned to face Lizzy. "When we enter the building, you will not say a word. I will do all the talking. No matter what I say, you will give no reaction. And stop messing with your wig."

"Sophia, you're scaring me." Lizzy pulled her hand away from her head as worry etched her big soulful eyes.

"Are my instructions clear?"

She nodded. "I won't say anything."

Lizzy tightened her coat around herself and followed beside me as we made our way to the doorman at the entrance of the building.

The man scanned Lizzy and my attire from head to toe, assessing whether or not we belonged here. Then, satisfied with his inspection, he tilted his head and opened the door.

"Good evening, ladies."

"Good evening." I shifted my glasses slightly to wink at him through my blue contacts. Then I ushered Lizzy forward before moving toward the security guard.

He stepped out from behind his station and asked, "Which residence are you expected at?"

"Randolph."

He narrowed his eyes. "Mr. Randolph normally notifies me of guests arriving."

"Give him a call. My orders were to make everything perfect for his arrival. You know how tired he gets after dealing with models all day." I leaned forward and ran my fingers up the guard's tie. "I'm sure you can explain why you disturbed his evening to confirm something he's arranged many times with you."

His eyes grew big. "You're from the agency."

"You could say that." I gestured to Lizzy and licked my lips. "It's a double-hitter night."

"Are others expected as well?"

"More than likely. We're just the set-up team

to welcome Mr. Randolph home before the party starts." I smiled up at him, making him flush. "Maybe I can convince him to invite you up. Would you like that?"

"Umm. I'm on duty."

"Well, come find me if the party is still on when you finish work. My name is Kellena."

He nodded, walked back to his station, and picked up a pen. "This code will grant you access to Mr. Randolph's floor. I'm sure you know, but he makes me remind everyone. Stay out of his studio."

I rose on tiptoes, taking the paper from the guard's fingers and pecking him on the cheek. "I'm interested in his other things, not his clothes. If you know what I mean?"

Taking Lizzy's hand, I tugged her to the elevator and stepped inside, punching in the code for Keith's floor.

As soon as the doors shut, Lizzy erupted. "Are you out of your mind? You let him believe we were prostitutes."

"Yep." I glanced at the watch on my wrist. "We have no more than thirty minutes before jackass, and his hookers arrive. I want him to see my handiwork."

"What are you about to do?"

"Show you what happens when an abusive asshole gets served some justice."

We arrived in the opulent foyer of Keith's apartment and, without knowing where I was going, decided to head left. I'd once heard the prick mention he liked the natural light on the left side of his apartment in the mornings and how he loved it, said it's where he did his best work.

"Bingo," I murmured to myself.

Unbuttoning my jacket, I shrugged it off and tossed it to Lizzy.

"You stay right there. I don't want you to be part of this."

Lizzy's attention turned to the design studio filled with fabrics, mannequins, and various garments in stages of completion. I dug into my pocket and pulled out a switchblade, flipping it open.

I loved this thing. Lucian had given it to me. I never really thought to use it until recently.

"Sophia, don't do anything rash."

"Lizzy, I told you this wasn't your scene. Now deal. I'm paying this asshole back for all the women he's hurt."

Opening the door to the studio, I began my assault on every piece of fabric I could grab, slicing and tearing. I shredded designs and sketches. I destroyed sets ready for upcoming shows. I wanted this bastard to suffer. I wanted him to pay for all the hurt he'd caused to girls like Alice and me.

I hate him. Now he'd know he wouldn't get away with it.

Grabbing a piece of paper, I wrote a note so he'd understand why this happened.

Touch anyone without consent again, and things will only get worse.

Lizzy banged on the glass door and shouted, "You've been in there too long. We have to go."

I checked the clock on the wall and cringed.

Fuck. I'd been in here nearly thirty minutes.

I scanned around me, making sure I hadn't left anything to link back to me. Then I rushed out.

"Let's go. We need to stop at a different floor and take the stairs."

"What do you mean?" The panic on Lizzy's face matched the worry now creeping up inside me.

"I went over time. We had thirty minutes before Keith's team would arrive to set up for his sex party. We have to go."

The elevator started moving before we reached it, and my stomach dropped. Searching around, I looked for the stairwell.

"I hope you're ready for some exercise." I pulled off my heels, and Lizzy followed my actions.

We made it to the emergency stairs. Using the security code, I unlocked it and made our way down to the main lobby. I'd barely set my hand on the door when I heard shouts about vandalism and to call security.

Breathing heavily, Lizzy and I pressed our backs to the wall.

"I don't think we should go through there," Lizzy advised. "We need to find a better way. What about the parking deck?"

"Let's go down a few more floors."

"Isn't there anyone you can call?"

I thought about it as we took another flight of stairs down.

Lucian. I'd call him. No judgment, no anger. He'd expect an explanation, and then he'd likely find my method too easy of a solution.

"I'll call Lucian."

Lizzy visibly relaxed.

Pulling out my phone, I dialed, but when the person answered, it wasn't Lucian's voice on the other end of the line.

"Sophia, what's wrong?"

"Damon...I...umm"

"Who's Damon? I thought you were calling Lucian." Lizzy nudged me.

"Sophia, answer me."

"It's okay. I called you by accident. I'll call Lucian."

"You will not hang up. What is the matter?"

"I—I need you to come to get my sister and me."

"Give me the address. I'm on my way."

✧ ✧ ✧

LESS THAN THIRTY minutes after my call to Damon, I spotted his sleek dark blue Maybach make a right near the cross-section where Lizzy and I remained hidden from public view.

An uneasiness churned in the pit of my stomach. For the hundredth time, I questioned why I'd dial Damon's number instead of Lucian's. My instinct should have pulled toward my brother. Still, it had settled on a man who, deep down, wanted nothing to do with me but couldn't stay away from me because of some unknown lure we seemed to have for each other.

Why couldn't I draw a line with this man?

Bringing him into this part of my life meant he knew more of my secrets and deeper parts of me, and I hadn't a clue about him outside of what I'd heard from others or the barest of things he'd told me. He kept his life very private, and what I had found about him online only gave very light information on how he and his brother and sister sold the corporation they'd inherited from their father within a year of his passing.

It made no sense why someone like him desired me so much. High profile and complicated were most Morelli's M.O.

Especially me.

I glanced at Lizzy, leaning against a pillar in the entryway to a closed coffee shop. Poor thing never expected the adventure I'd taken her on. No matter how much she believed she could handle things, she remained innocent of life in general.

I wanted it that way. My baby sister deserved to have some of her purity and innocence preserved. At least with the older of us taking the brunt of the terror of our father and the distance of our mother, she'd been spared the overall trauma we'd endured.

"Don't think I'm not going to ply you with questions later."

Lizzy eyed me with what I assumed was her

attempt at a disapproving glare. Still, the exhaustion from the evening's events erased any of the impact.

"I wouldn't expect anything less. Just wait until we get back to my place."

"I thought you said we couldn't go back there tonight," worry crept into Lizzy's voice.

"We will lay low at Damon's place."

"Does he know this?"

I cringed inside. "I'm assuming so since I expect he'll want all the details of our escapades."

"Who is he to you?"

"I don't know. I'm still trying to figure it out." Damon's car pulled to a stop, and I grabbed Lizzy's hand and guided her in his direction.

She followed me without uttering a word. However, her eyes scanned everywhere and took in every detail of the vehicle and the man behind the steering wheel.

Before we reached the car, Damon stepped out and opened the back passenger door.

"Good evening, ladies. Lisbetta, please have a seat. Sophia, in the front with me."

His tone brooked no argument, and immediately, both of us followed his directions.

I'd barely closed the door when he moved into traffic. He remained quiet, letting the silence build on the already thick tension growing between us.

I glanced his way a few times, hoping he'd say something, but he kept his attention on the road.

When we arrived at a stunning high-rise, I couldn't help but admire the structure.

"Did you design it?"

"Among other things."

I cocked my head, glaring at him, but instead of retorting with a smartass remark, I opened the car door and stepped out, not waiting for the attendant.

I focused my attention on a discreet plaque and scanned the names of the businesses housed in the building. All of them bore the Pierce name in one fashion or the other.

Damon worked and lived in the same building.

No work-life balance, it seemed.

Was that why he went to the club? To give him that separation, the relief from the intensity of his life. No, the intensity was an ingrained part of him. Something one couldn't separate from the man.

"Sophia, let's go." Damon touched my lower back, pulling me from my thoughts.

He led Lizzy and me to an elevator that took

us directly into a vast, expansive foyer of windows overlooking the city.

He designed the space to wow anyone arriving at his home. But, at the same time, it also gave a separation from the rest of the penthouse.

"How long have you lived here?"

"A little over a year."

An unexpected surge of relief shot through me, knowing his former submissive hadn't been with him here. Why did it matter? It didn't. No, that wasn't true, but there was no point thinking about it now.

Pushing my unnecessary emotions back, I said, "It's impressive."

"I believe so." He smirked, then the expression on his face grew concerned, and I looked toward Lizzy.

She clutched her coat around her, shaking as if cold overwhelmed her sinking deep into her bones.

"Lizzy, it's going to be okay," I tried to reassure her. "You're crashing from the adrenaline surge. Once you get some sleep, you'll feel fine."

Lizzy nodded, taking a step, but stumbled. Damon maneuvered around me and then lifted Lizzy into his arms.

"I believe your adventure has taken its toll on

her. Let's get her settled. Afterward, we need to have a private discussion."

Fifteen minutes later, after ensuring Lizzy was fast asleep, I joined Damon in his living room. The cityscape illuminated him in shadow, adding to the foreboding mood.

His dark green gaze lifted to mine. "What kind of trouble are you in, Sophia?"

"I'm not in trouble." I pursed my lips. "You came to get me. Problem solved."

"Your problems have only begun."

My heartbeat accelerated. "Are you planning on punishing me?"

The way heat flared in his irises, I wasn't sure whether I should run or not.

"That depends on your answer to this question."

"And that is?"

"Why did you call me Sophia?"

"I have no damn idea." I shook my head. "No, that's not true. I trust you, and I feel safe with you. So without thinking, I dialed you and not Lucian."

He gestured to the sofa. "I want you to sit down and tell me everything that happened tonight and all that led up to it."

I nodded, not knowing where to start. I'd

never shared any of this with anyone. Could I go there? Could I relive the memories and reasons why I hated Keith so damn much?

I lifted my gaze and stared into Damon's green ones. He watched me patiently as if he sensed I needed to gather my thoughts.

With a deep breath, I began, "My unwanted career as a tabloid headliner started all because of a lie created by Keith Randolph."

I paused, waiting for a reaction, but he gave me none, so I continued.

"From childhood, I'd never fit the mold of a perfect Morelli daughter. Nothing anyone said nor the various types of discipline thrown my way could make me conform to the rules set out for me."

"What do you mean discipline?"

I smirked. "Didn't Lucian tell you about Bryant Morelli's forms of discipline? Once he and Leo moved out, the remaining troublemaker in the house faced many challenges."

Anger washed over Damon's face. "Your mother didn't protect you?"

"She couldn't even protect herself. Besides, her place in society mattered more than finding ways to shelter her children from her husband's wrath." I shook my head. "That isn't the story I want to tell tonight."

"Okay. How does your past tie to tonight."

"Around the time I turned eighteen, a designer who'd made a few custom gowns for my family asked if I'd walk in his runway show. Immediately, my parents refused, saying modeling wasn't something a girl from polite society picked as a career."

"Let me guess, you went behind their backs and accepted."

I couldn't help but smile. "It was childish, I know, but it was also my fuck you to my parents for trying to control every aspect of my life. I hadn't expected it to lead to an agency deal and multiple shoots."

I tucked a stray hair behind my ear and curled my feet underneath me on the sofa. "Then, not six months later, I was invited to walk the runway for an up-and-coming designer who thought I was the perfect shape for his creations. My agent said it was a great opportunity for me and that he planned to create a piece with me in mind. I was his new muse or some bullshit."

"Let me guess, Randolph."

Instead of confirming, I kept talking, "He had a reputation for dating his muses and assumed I'd jump at the chance. During a fitting, he asked me out, but I told him I didn't have time to date with my schedule. He seemed fine with it, and I never thought about it. I should have known better. An hour after I walked his show, he locked me in a back dressing room."

Closing my eyes, I dropped my head. In the next second, Damon tucked me against his chest with his arms wrapped around me tight.

"If I hadn't used the self-defense moves Lucian forced me to learn to get away, he would have done so much more to me. That very night, he retaliated by having pictures taken of me leaving a building where he'd orchestrated a drug-filled celebrity party. All I'd done was spend the night at a friend's place, crying my eyes out and feeling so helpless."

"Okay. Now I need you to tell me how your assault connects to tonight."

"He continued to corner other girls after me. Recently, I found one of his victims. No girl should ever feel that way. No girl should ever have her choices taken from her. No girl should ever feel so vulnerable. He threatened her with his power, money, and influence if she told a soul. He'd done the same thing to me. In the end, he ruined my reputation to get my compliance."

I finally explained what I did this evening in

Keith's penthouse and the reasons why.

"So you destroyed his studio and featured pieces for his collection to make a point?"

"I wanted him to know that every time he touches someone, there is a price to pay." Bile burned the back of my throat, having to relive the memories and recount the details of the past few years. "I hate that man. He was the catalyst for everything."

A tear slipped down my cheek.

"Do you know what it feels like to have your own mother believe you're a pill-popping whore over asking if any of the rumors were true? Or even once, just questioning the validity of the reports? Her standing in society is all that matters to her, the lovers she thinks I don't know about, and putting up with Dad's abuse, so she keeps the lifestyle she adores so fucking much."

The pain rose inside me as if it had waited for me to set it free.

"I was eighteen when that bastard cornered me. He'd made me ashamed and convinced me that I deserved it, especially after the fallout he'd created. What I wouldn't have given to have one person tell me it wasn't my fault, that what happened to me was the act of a predator. I wanted Alice to know someone would avenge her." I stared at Damon's stony face, which gave away none of his thoughts. "Until I met you, the last time I cried was when Dad told me at eighteen that he'd washed his hands of me with my antics. You love my tears. I fucking hate them."

Damon cupped my cheek. "You aren't weak for releasing your emotions. You're strong and fierce. Seeing you let go is a gift."

"Don't say things like that. It confuses me."

What I kept inside was the thought that it made me want things I knew he couldn't give me.

"What are you confused about?"

"You make me feel things, and I refuse to become a woman dependent on any man."

"You fear becoming your mother."

"I refuse to become her." I clenched my jaw. "Whatever this thing is between us, Damon Pierce. I'll never let it take over my life. I'll walk away the second I see it happening."

"Then I guess we don't have anything to worry about."

"I guess we don't."

He leaned down and then kissed my forehead. I lifted my face to capture his lips, but he pulled back. The depth and hunger in his gaze ignited a throbbing deep in my pussy.

Even after all I'd confessed, all I'd revealed, all my mind told me I shouldn't do, my body yearned for his touch. I'd grown addicted to him in a way I knew only led to disaster.

"Now I have three words for you."

The press of his cock stayed a heady presence underneath me, making it hard to concentrate.

"Okay."

"Go to bed." He released me and helped me to stand.

A heavy lump formed in my stomach, and all the arousal from moments ago disappeared.

"I assume I will share the room with Lizzy?"

"Unless you've changed your mind about your status as a submissive."

I shook my head. "No."

He was drawing a line, wanting to know if I'd cross it, testing me. This man held a power over my body unlike anyone I'd encountered before, but I refused to let that rule me.

We stared at each other for a few seconds, and then he nodded. "You're right. It's better this way."

So now he accepted my decision. For fuck's sake.

"What made this sudden change of heart? Is it because I don't bend to your will like the other women you've encountered?"

"It's better for you to view things in that manner." He smirked with a calculated gleam. "However, let me clear something up. If I will it, I can have you on your knees right now, ready to suck my cock."

My core clenched with the thought of it, and I clenched my jaw.

"You think so?"

"I know so. Would you like to know why I'm not using this draw, as you call it, to change your mind?"

I swayed a bit toward him before I gained control of myself. "Go ahead and tell me."

"Because I'd fuck you and physically please you, but in the end, I wouldn't give you the one thing you need. For both our sakes, we need to move on altogether."

"I see."

"No, you don't." He shook his head. "It's more about what's the least selfish thing to do on my part. I enjoy my solitude and privacy. I don't do galas or shows. I don't give two shits about making appearances. Pick someone comfortable in your high-profile life. It's not me."

Pain shot through my heart. Another fucking person decided to use my life to reject me.

I kept my face void of emotion when I asked, "Are you protecting yourself or me?"

"You. I'm already damned."

Fuck him with that cop-out statement.

I moved in the direction of Lizzy's room, pausing for a brief moment to say, "We shouldn't see each other again, in or out of the club. Thank you for helping me tonight."

CHAPTER THIRTEEN

Damon

SHE COULDN'T POSSIBLY enjoy this life.

I thought to myself as I entered the rooftop nightclub of one of the top boutique hotels in New York City, four days after Sophia's B&E incident.

Two mogul musicians had rented the entire establishment for an extravagant party with attendees invited from anyone considered on the A-list, especially those in Hollywood, music, and fashion. The event commemorated the launch of the musical duo's new clothing line during fashion week.

The crowd shouted and danced, some half-naked and others stoned or drunk. No one seemed to care about the copious amounts of drugs openly used or distributed among the partygoers. All that mattered was that everyone had a great time.

On a long sofa sat one of the models that

Sophia had walked the runway with a few days earlier. She looked barely coherent, with her head lolled back and eyes glazed. The person next to her offered her a drink and then a joint.

A third person pulled out a lighter to give the model her fist hit.

That couldn't be healthy.

The thought of Sophia putting herself in these types of situations infuriated me, and a surge of anger coursed through my body. She deserved so much better, so much more.

During her confession, she'd said she rarely drank unless she was in a safe space, but what if an asshole slipped something into her water or soft drink at one of these events. She'd end up like that model or worse.

I wanted her locked away in my penthouse, protected from scum like this. I'd take care of her, keep her safe. She'd want for nothing. Pleasure, pain, everything she ever desired, I'd provide.

What the hell was I thinking? I had to snap out of it.

My attention shifted from the groups around me as a door near the bar opened, and a tall blond man stepped out while wiping his nose, followed by three women. He laughed and joked and then returned to the room.

There he was. The fucking son of a bitch.

He'd put his hands on her.

My Sophia.

He'd destroyed a part of her that she'd never get back.

Stalking toward the corner of the club, I turned the doorknob as soon as I approached it and entered the room. Keith Randolph leaned over a glass table, snorting up what I assumed was either cocaine or heroin.

Fucking idiot. All the money in the world, and he'd instead fry his brain like that.

"Who the fuck are you?" he asked, barely lifting his head as he finished his line of white powder.

"I'm here to deliver a message."

He wiped his face on his sleeve and then scanned me up and down. "You're no messenger wearing a suit worth more than ten grand."

At least I could give it to him that he knew custom-designed clothing.

"Oh, but I am." I stepped closer to him. "How did your show go the other day?"

"I knew it. That bitch did it." He clenched his jaw.

"Do you want to elaborate on what you know? And referring to women in such a manner isn't something I appreciate hearing."

"Her family sent you. Didn't they?"

"Let's get more specific."

"Fucking Morelli. That whore. Does she have any idea how much she cost me?"

I grabbed him by the shirt, hurling him forward. "What makes you believe anyone named Morelli sent me? From what I hear, you don't understand the meaning of consent."

He clung to my wrist and shoved against my hold, but his strength was no match for mine. For a man near my height and build, the drugs and party lifestyle made him weak.

He wasn't so tough when it came to someone his own size. However, he had plenty of strength against those smaller than him, especially defenseless women.

"What the hell did she tell you? She fucking spread her legs the minute she saw me. She wanted to be in the limelight. That's how they all are. You don't know the industry. I do."

A rage like nothing I'd experienced before boiled inside me. The visions of ripping this asshole's head from his body inundated my mind.

How dare this piece of shit soil her name in this way.

I lifted him by the throat, nearly cutting off

his air supply. "You like to slut shame women into complying with your demands. That makes you a pathetic asshole in my book. I looked you up. What happened when you were in high school?"

"None of it is true. The judge dismissed the case." He gasped and whimpered.

Because Daddy had it expunged, and then they destroyed the family of the girl who'd brought allegations against him.

Families like the Randolphs mistakenly believed they could cover up crimes because of their wealth. They forgot buying off the families never cleared memories of former employees, bank or hospital records, or local gossip.

When Sophia divulged her story, I knew Keith Randolph hadn't started his predatory behavior once he moved to New York City to become a designer. Minutes after Sophia left me to sleep, I'd called my private investigator to gather information. By morning, he'd given me more than I expected.

"Her brothers retaliated and left you in the hospital. But you never revealed the attackers because they found a video you kept as a souvenir of your assault on their sister." I leaned forward. "Your father paid them off to keep said recording from going public. Or is that not true either?"

Fear entered his eyes as well as comprehension.

"How did you find any of this out?"

I narrowed my gaze. "You're worried about how I found out and not the fact I am going to end you?"

"Who are you?"

"You touched someone recently, didn't you? Maybe I'm her brother. Did you consider that?"

He shook his head in confusion. "Alice only has sisters. It's that fucking cunt, Morelli. I know it. Her family is the only one capable of this."

I slammed the bastard into a nearby wall, making him scream as his head jarred against the plaster.

"Never. And I mean, never refer to Sophia or any female in that manner again. Did you or did you not corner an innocent seventeen-year-old girl in a bathroom three days ago?"

"I… I…"

"Answer me, or I will eliminate you right here, and no one will care. By the time this party is over, a cleanup crew will come in, and there will be no evidence of your existence."

"She flirted with me, so I showed her I was open, and then she started screaming and cr—"

he gurgled, stopping his next words as I squeezed his neck in a debilitating grip.

"If you ever touch another woman without consent, you will die. If you ever go near Alice Stansbury or do anything to ruin her reputation, you will die. And if you so much as look in Sophia Morelli's direction, you won't just die. I will take great pleasure in ensuring the time beforehand is long and painful where you will wish and beg for me to end it."

That's when I heard water drip, and I glanced down to see the front of Keith's pants soaked and urine pooling underneath his feet.

"Do I have your agreement?"

He whimpered and then nodded. "Yes. I won't go near them or look at them."

"If I discover you did anything to harm them or any other woman, I will make you regret it."

"I—I promise. I won't do anything."

I threw him on the floor, stepping back. Randolph curled into a ball.

"Fucking pathetic."

The adrenaline and fury burned inside me, and I knew if I stayed any longer, I'd go past threats and carry out the vengeance I sought.

I stared at the crumpled form of the man who'd hurt Sophia.

This cowering waste of space deserved no less than to have my hands ripping him limb from limb and bathe my fingers in his blood.

Every nerve in my body shook to destroy him.

Turning, I opened the door and headed out of the club and the hotel.

Keeping my breaths steady, I pushed down the nausea stirring in my gut. This bloodlust coursing through my veins was unlike anything I'd experienced before. I craved more of it. I hungered to revel in this feeling.

Sophia Morelli was the reason I wanted more and more.

The woman consumed me, filled me with the need to salt the earth with the bones of any man who dared hurt her.

✧ ✧ ✧

FORTY-FIVE MINUTES LATER, I stepped into the lounge of Violent Delights with my emotions no calmer than when I'd left the bastard Randolph in the nightclub.

The best thing for me was to lose myself to someone other than Sophia Morelli. I would find a sub with experience who loved pain and understood the rules, a beauty without dark hair or midnight eyes, to whom I wouldn't have to teach every damn thing.

I circled the lounge, studying the couples, groups, and individuals at the tables, gathering spots, and sofas. The place was at capacity tonight, giving the space a hedonistic atmosphere.

As I moved toward the bar, a few subs I'd entertained and enjoyed in the past sat in a social circle in a corner, passing glances my way and giving the signal of interest. They were beautiful, loved pain, and understood what I expected, but sadly, none stirred the desire in me to take them up on their offer.

I approached the bartender Tate, who pushed my customary soft drink in my direction with an incline of his head. Taking the glass, I downed half the contents and let the cool liquid soothe my parched throat.

Most people would have chosen a more potent beverage, especially with the mood that simmered in my blood. However, they hadn't grown up with someone who overindulged on a regular basis. I'd lived thirty-five years without touching the stuff, and I'd survive the rest of my life not having partaken in the oblivion alcohol offered.

My vices lay in other realms, such as this place. The cries, the moans, the fucking tears from desire, pain, pleasure, I craved it, wanted it, needed it.

I scanned the room again, my gaze connecting with a sultry brunette relaxing on a chaise. Everything about her was perfect, a beautiful face, large breasts, voluptuous curves, plump lips, and her wristband marked her as an experienced sub who enjoyed pain.

She'd let me tie her, beat her, fuck her, and we'd both walk away satisfied.

The brunette shifted in her seat, giving me an inviting smile.

Not a fucking spark.

My cock only wanted Sophia Morelli.

The woman I'd pushed away.

Her moans. Her pleas. Her whimpers. Her fucking pain and those damn beautiful tears.

Gritting my teeth, I set the glass on the bar top and walked out of the lounge.

CHAPTER FOURTEEN

Sophia

SOPHIA MORELLI – ELITE MODEL OR HIGH-END SOMETHING ELSE?

I STARED AT the headline on the screen of my phone wishing for nothing more than to hide under the covers of my bed and never come out.

According to multiple outlets, I made a name for myself in the fashion industry by sleeping my way to the top. And to add insult to injury, in a few articles, allegedly my friends and I positioned ourselves for the top jobs in a manner that made us nothing but elite escorts.

That fucking bastard.

There was no doubt in my mind, in every fiber of my being, that Keith Randolph was behind this. He had so much money and time, and he wasted it on me, making my life hell instead of working on his fashion house with its subpar line of clothing.

How had he figured out it was me?

Since the night two weeks ago when Lizzy and I visited Keith's penthouse, I'd consistently checked the reports and used my connections to find out who they suspected as the intruders. According to the police report, they believed the culprits among a list of models Keith had publicly humiliated during the fashion week selection process.

Having a well-known reputation for being an asshole left a large pool of conspirators.

He'd been correct in fixating on me, but that was beside the point. In the grand scheme of things, I hadn't interacted with the bastard in years. Whenever possible, I avoided being in the same building with him.

Then again, I should have expected him to come for me. Of all the people he'd fucked with over the years, the only one who'd have any ability to fight back was me.

We, Morellis, had our underworld connections, after all. If only I'd thought to use them.

The fucking nerve of the asshole.

He utilized the services of escorts and now trashed me as one—misogynistic asshole.

Turning off my screen, I swallowed down the worry and terror of what I'd face when I stepped outside my apartment and made my way to my kitchen.

Yeah, it was one in the afternoon, but a girl needed something to calm the hell down. I searched through my cabinets and shelves, finding nothing but mineral water.

Where were all the wine and bottles of liquor I kept around for guests?

Then I thought for a second. Lizzy had a key to my place and had strolled right in that day. That sneaky little… She stole all my alcohol.

I guessed I couldn't hold it against her too much. I had scared the shit out of her with the Keith incident.

I'd checked up on her every day, and she insisted she had a new respect for my lady balls, but I still wasn't convinced she'd recovered from all the excitement. As the youngest of us, we'd done all we could to protect and preserve her innocence. That was until I nearly got her into the biggest trouble of her life.

Dread settled in my gut, thinking about what could have happened to us and what I'd face with this new shit spreading about me.

How would I explain this? Only the small circle of people who truly knew me wouldn't believe a word of these new lies, but the public had already latched on.

Oh God, oh God, oh God.

I'd survived worse.

People believed I'd snorted drugs and danced on tables at eighteen.

I'd made it through then. I could deal with this now.

A series of texts bombarded my phone, and I couldn't muster the energy to scan them. More beeps chimed, and then the sound of an incoming call filled the air.

I dropped my head on the kitchen counter, allowing the coolness from the stone to penetrate the heat of the skin on my forehead.

For a split second, I thought of calling Eva, wanting a big sister's advice, but decided against it. The last thing she needed was to add my drama to her life while pregnant and planning a wedding.

Constantly alone in a crisis, without a soul to call on for support or to hold me for comfort.

I closed my eyes, remembering that Damon had been there for me as I told him about Keith. He'd held me. I'd felt safe, wrapped in his arms.

He'd helped me that night. Could I reach out to him again?

No, that was a bad idea.

I wouldn't see him again. I'd made the decision. I'd handle this as I dealt with everything else. One day at a time.

The second the ringing stopped, it started up again. With a sigh, I reached for my cell. The display showed my father's number.

I hesitated for a moment and then answered, "Hello."

"Sophia, get to the house now," Dad ordered, anger lacing his every word. "There is a car downstairs. Come straight to my office."

He hung up before I had a chance to respond.

Would he slap me or reprimand me? One never knew. Leo took the brunt of the discipline when we were younger, but on occasion, the rest of us earned our fair share of Dad's wrath.

And, of course, Mom stood by with her lectures of how disappointed she was in my life's choices between preparations for the next social event.

I closed my eyes, taking in a few breaths to center myself. One day, I'd find a way out of this anger, this resentment for parents who never cared.

If only I had the resolve of my older siblings. They found their way without needing anyone's approval.

Grabbing my purse and jacket, I squared my

shoulders and headed out of my apartment.

✧ ✧ ✧

ARRIVING AT MY parent's place felt like I'd already endured days of battle. I sighed in relief, unbuttoned my coat, and then took the long hallway leading to Dad's office.

The moment I'd stepped out of the elevator, a group of reporters swarmed me.

They'd bombarded me with questions about the rumors.

"Are you a call girl?"

"Did you sleep with the listed designers?"

"Are you a madam or one of the workers?"

I kept my head up, ignored everyone, and pushed through the crowd until I reached the driver Dad sent for me.

How the fuck they'd managed to sneak past the security in my building, I wouldn't know. But one thing was for sure. It would never happen again. I'd sent a message to Lucian about the incident, and he instructed that he'd handle it.

I'd mastered the art of acting the part of the uncaring, wild child Morelli heiress. The paparazzi knew I wouldn't answer them by now, but they had to try.

Just as I'd slid into the car, one reporter asked,

"Is it true you got on your knees in more ways than one to be his muse when you were eighteen?"

It had taken all my strength not to respond. I knew it was the columnists' job to push my buttons for the headlines, but it would have been nice to punch a motherfucker in the face. Lucky for me, the Morelli training won out over my rage.

As I approached Dad's office door, I heard his booming voice reverberate through the wood. Whoever he spoke to, anger laced every one of his words.

Wonderful. Just the environment I wanted to enter when expecting an ass-chewing.

Steeling myself for whatever was to come, I knocked.

"Come in."

Turning the handle, I stepped inside to see Dad's stern gaze pierce mine and my mother sitting in the chair on the other side of the desk.

"At least you can follow instructions for once."

Saying nothing, I closed the door behind me and waited.

"What the hell is the meaning of this?" He gestured to his computer monitor. "Do you have any dignity? Do you have any honor? Don't you think our family name already has enough soiling it with your brothers' antics only to add your mess to it?"

He shifted as if to step around his desk, and I braced for him to stalk over and slap me.

"Don't you have anything to say for yourself, or are you just going to stand there?"

I swallowed and replied, "Would you believe me if I said none of it is true?"

Mom shook her head, and her shoulders slumped as if utter disappointment washed over her. Inside, a crushing sadness engulfed me. Even now, she couldn't even consider my innocence.

"Why would anyone make this up about you?"

Anger surged inside me. "Did you think it was because I wouldn't sleep with them? That I wouldn't let them put their hands on me? Men like to retaliate when they don't get their way."

"Who?" Dad moved in my direction, gripping my upper arms. "Give me his name."

"It doesn't matter, Dad."

"If it's true, then give me the name." He shook me.

I narrowed my gaze and lifted my chin. "I needed you to ask about the truth years ago. It doesn't matter now. Didn't you and Mom wash your hands of me long ago?"

"Do you care nothing about our family name?"

"Not really."

My mother gasped. "Sophia, do you have any concept of how this scandal will overshadow Eva's wedding?"

What was so wrong with me that I kept holding on to the hope that they would one day love me?

I jerked out of Dad's hold and stared at my parents. "You two are unbelievable."

Sophia, you are twenty-five fucking years old. It's time to grow the hell up and accept your reality.

"Sophia. Watch your tone." The anger radiating from Dad matched mine.

I had no fucks left to give.

What would Lucian do? What would Leo do? They'd give it to Dad and Mom straight.

Well, that's what I'd do.

I stepped toward the door, holding myself with as much strength as possible, and asked, "Why did you two have so many children if you only care about your name and place in society?"

"You do not question how I run my family. When you start contributing, then we can talk.

Right now, all you do is cause problems."

Frustration and sadness burned the back of my throat.

"Don't worry. I'll handle this like everything else. On my own. You and the family will come out unscathed as usual."

I turned the handle and left the room as fast as possible. I only had seconds before Dad exploded on me, and if he really lost it, he'd chase after me to make his point. The man loved to have the last word, and I refused to let him win.

Why the fuck should I? I conformed to no one.

I turned the corner in the direction of the parlor room and collided straight into Lucian, knocking my head straight into his chin.

"Oh shit. I'm so sorry." I grabbed onto Lucian's forearms as he steadied me and adjusted his balance.

Lucian looked behind me, utterly unfazed by the fact I smacked into his face. "Who are you running from, Sophia?"

"It doesn't matter. Can we get out of here? I want to go home."

"Since you're the person I came here for, let's go."

"How did you know I was here?"

"Where else would you be after a morning of headline-making scandals?"

I clenched my jaw. "None of it is true."

"It never is." He studied me. "Time to spill all of your secrets, Sophia. I want to know what started this and why you didn't come to me in the first place?"

✧   ✧   ✧

"START TALKING," LUCIAN commanded the moment his driver turned the street away from our parents' house in Bishop's Landing.

Lucian unbuttoned his jacket, cocked an arm over the back of the seat, and then patiently waited for me to begin.

We were the two outsiders in the family, the nonconformist, the troublemakers. Often, I'd wonder what it had been like for him growing up. I'd heard stories about how Dad had adored him and then hated him.

At least if Dad hated me, there would be some emotion toward me. I wasn't even sure if he felt anything for me. I was a thing, an accomplishment, a checkmark in a book. Something he showed the priest at mass to say look, I completed another duty in God's name by continuing my family line.

Shit. There I went again. I really needed that drink.

Scanning the car, I frowned when I realized there wasn't a bottle or tumbler in sight.

Lucian noticed my reaction and commented, "Problems?"

My shoulders sagged. "I don't even know where to start."

"I'm not going to pull teeth to get the answers. Give it to me straight. How much trouble are you in?"

"If the cops link the crime to me, then a lot."

Lucian lifted a brow and glared at me. "Keep going. I want all of it."

I thought of Damon and how I'd given him the story. Now here I sat with Lucian, the very person I should have called in the first place that night.

One thing I knew for sure, today's issues would never have happened because Lucian would have killed Keith and dumped his body somewhere. Dead men couldn't orchestrate tabloid fodder.

But then again, I hated the idea of anything linking back to anyone I cared about.

Releasing a deep breath, I relayed an almost mythological recounting of events.

"He deserved more than what I did to his stupid clothes." I tried to gauge Lucian's thoughts, but he kept his face impassive. "I wanted to burn his place down."

"You have brothers to exact the damage necessary for people like him."

"I wanted to be the one to execute justice."

He cocked his head to the side. "What are you leaving out?"

"Security nearly caught us, and I called—" I hesitated for a second and said, "a friend to get us."

"You called a friend? Doing a job with another person was bad enough, but a fucking friend, an outsider before one of us?" The outrage in his question told me how much I'd fucked up. "This shit stays in the family. Whenever you need help, call one of your brothers."

"I intended to call you, but I didn't realize I dialed Damon until he answered."

"You called Damon? Are you kidding me?" Lucian shifted his body to face me, irritation blazing in his dark eyes.

"What?" I couldn't hide my confusion.

"What's going on with you two?"

I folded my arms across my body. "It's none of your business."

"The hell it isn't. You're my sister. I have all the say in the world."

"Did I ever ask you about all the women you slept with before you met Elaine?"

"The hold he has on you is dangerous. I won't fucking have it."

"He doesn't have any hold on me. I called him, and he picked us up. We spent the night at his place and then left the next morning. That's it. I haven't seen him since."

"That's it, my ass." He ran a frustrated hand through his hair.

"If you're talking about his submissive that killed herself, you don't need to worry about me. I'm not expecting anything from Damon."

"You say that now, but I've watched it happen with all of his past women. They fall for him to the point of obsession. They will beg for any attention he'll give them because when he is with them, he makes them feel as if they are the center of his world."

"Are you saying he uses them and throws them away?"

"That's the thing. Damon Pierce never lies. He is brutally honest and upfront with every one of them. They know love isn't part of the equation. They know he won't ever pick them in the middle of a crowd as some grand gesture. And every one of them thinks they are the one to change him and get him to fall in love. I refuse to let you become the next name on that list."

"As I said, you don't need to worry about me. I already decided not to see him again."

Surprise flashed in his eyes. "What brought you to make that decision?"

"No matter how intense things got between us, he never truly dropped his guard. He knew so much more about me than I did about him. There was no balance. I'm worth so much more than a man who pushes me away every time guilt overwhelms him about his deceased sub. I'm not her and won't live in her shadow."

Pride lit Lucian's eyes, and then he nodded and smiled. "You think like a woman who knows her worth."

It took all my strength not to burst into tears. For the first time in my life, someone saw me as more than a fuckup.

"Living away from the family taught me many hard lessons."

"You come to me in the future. Is that understood?"

"Is there a future for Keith, or are you planning to pay him a visit?"

"First, I'll need to pay Pierce a visit and punch him in the face for setting this shit with Randolph in motion."

I frowned. "What does any of my issues have to do with Damon?"

"Let's put two and two together. You told the man who claimed you in the middle of my club that someone assaulted you, ruined your reputation, and then continued to do the same shit to other women. What do you think that man will do after hearing said information?"

It took me a few seconds to wrap my mind around Lucian's question.

There were jokes in some fashion circuits about Keith having his ass handed to him last week by an irritated boyfriend at a party. I'd blown it off and taken it as wishful thinking. Plus, the people who shared the gossip belonged to the group that Keith had embarrassed before fashion week, so they weren't the most reliable sources.

Now, it made sense with everything going on and how Keith set everything up.

A shiver slid down my spine. "What did Damon do that caused this type of retaliation?"

"Something well deserved, I can assume." Lucian shook his head. "However, because Pierce left the idiot breathing, you're in this situation."

I stared at my brother as if he'd lost his mind.

"Are you listening to yourself?"

"You know who and what we are, Sophia. This vigilante shit you attempted and failed at says you're no better."

"I didn't fail at it." I folded my arms across my body. "I got the job done."

"Then called a man with a psychotic need to protect to come and pick you up."

"How would you react if someone hurt Elaine?"

The way his face hardened, I almost regretted asking the question.

"You already know the answer to that question, so why ask?"

We grew quiet, and then Lucian asked, "Will you see him now that you know he went to protect your honor?"

"No." I shook my head. "I won't become Mom. I won't take scraps as she does. I'd rather be alone than be her."

"Sophia, you're never going to be like her. You feel too damn much."

CHAPTER FIFTEEN

Damon

LEANING A FOREARM on a balcony railing, I surveyed the crowd gathered in the vestibule below me. They all waited for the hosts of the evening to make speeches and usher the guests into the space designated for the dining room.

Balls, parties, grand openings, and society events—they were all the same.

People pretended to enjoy each other's company for various purposes, ranging from connections, deals, marriages, introductions, etc. Most of them were inauthentic. The press, politicians, and celebrities circulated among millionaires and billionaires in the guise of a charity or celebration.

Tonight's being the dedication and grand opening of a building I'd designed and had an integral part in developing.

If not for my involvement in this project, I'd have stayed home, away from the chaos and her.

Fucking Sophia Morelli.

Surrounded by her parents and siblings, she stood out among their elegant style and appropriate attire.

Wearing some avant-garde art creation designed to accentuate all of her curves, she pushed the boundaries of what society deemed acceptable. The back of her gown displayed an intricate mix of sheer fabric, beading, and other textiles designed to construct the image of a dragon guarding his treasure of jewels—all black, of course.

She held herself in her usual "I don't give a fuck" fashion, making her more alluring to any male who happened to garner a glance.

Maybe that was why Bryant Morelli couldn't stop glaring at his daughter every time he glanced in her direction. But, from what I'd learned, he played happy family whenever in public, never giving any indication the Morellis were anything less than a united front.

With the ire he directed at Sophia, she'd done something to piss him off, more than likely in public.

And hence the reason, outside of business-related content, I'd avoided all other forms of social media or news for the last week or so. Any glimpse or information about Sophia would have pushed me to seek her out and break the vow I'd made to myself to stay away from her.

Now here I fucking was, ready to tear the head from the next man who decided to look at her for more than a few seconds.

I wanted her with every fiber of my being. She haunted me day and night, and doing the right thing, no longer appealed in the slightest.

No other woman would do.

I'd never comprehend how an inexperienced virgin had twisted my mind to this degree. But the idea of anyone else ever acquiring even the slightest taste of her gave me a vision of ripping a man's head off.

I craved to push her into a corner, run my hand up the long slit over her leg, and then destroy that sweet pussy until she gave me those beautiful tears of hers.

She'd gotten into my blood, and I wanted to consume her thoughts in the same way she'd invaded mine.

At that very moment, her attention shifted from her sister, Eva. She scanned the periphery of the area and then moved up until her gaze connected with mine.

Her mouth parted for the briefest of seconds,

and a slight flush crept up her cheeks.

My cock grew hard and painful with the lust staring directly at me. The visceral draw we shared almost seemed like a living, breathing thing.

Physically, I wanted her to a painful level, but there was this need to protect her, cherish her, keep her.

She reached to grab a drink from a passing server, downed the contents in the tumbler, and then licked her lips.

Continuing to hold my gaze, she set the glass on a nearby table. She smirked before mouthing, "refreshing water," and turned her back to me.

Even now, she played the brat.

I couldn't help but smile. Never had a woman gotten me to find humor in the things that would have annoyed me with anyone else. That flirty defiance made me want to bend her over the nearest surface and fuck her senseless.

"Give me one good reason why I shouldn't end you for the shit you stirred up for Sophia?" Lucian strolled up along the balcony adjacent to me, annoyance etched all over his face.

"I'm staying away from her as you wanted. What the hell have I done now?"

"Did you or did you not do a piss-poor job of handling Randolph?"

"I handled him. He won't mess with Sophia or anyone."

"Just because you made him piss his pants doesn't mean he listened."

Sliding my hand in my pocket, I adjusted my stance to face him. "How the fuck do you know that happened?"

"His circle of friends isn't as loyal when it comes to keeping embarrassing information quiet. Hence, the reason he retaliated against Sophia for your sloppy work."

Slow anger boiled inside me. "What did that piece of shit do to Sophia?"

"Even people who like solitude check the news for things other than business once in a while. Why don't you check the latest highlights on my sister? Then you'll know."

I pulled out my phone and typed Sophia's name into the search engine. My hands shook as I scrolled through an almost unending list of articles discussing Sophia, her friends, and links to alleged illicit relationships with designers, agents, and executives.

"This is all bullshit." I couldn't hide the rage in my voice.

That fucker thought I was kidding when I issued my threat. He had no idea the type of hell he'd just opened up for himself and his entire family.

Then again, maybe Lucian had done the job for me, and my plans to fuck up Randolph's life weren't necessary.

I looked up at Lucian. "Tell me you took care of him."

"No. I haven't touched him."

"Why the fuck not?"

"Since you created the mess, it's your job to get your hands dirty, and clean it the fuck up." His dark eyes narrowed. "Then again, it never came naturally to you, did it?"

I clenched my jaw. "Tell that to Maria's brother. He'd disagree with your assessment."

"You want to go there?"

"You seem to, so why not."

"Who saved your martyr ass that night?"

"I didn't ask you to do anything? You stuck your Morelli nose into my business."

"As if I'd leave you hanging, especially when you were too damn stupid to see her brother was just as culpable as you."

"I would have taken the fall. I deserved it."

"Maybe. But that's not how we work. Favor for a favor, or did you forget our deal?"

I shook my head. "Asshole. You act all mean

and shit. Then come in all white knight style."

"Fuck off with that. Whose construction sites handle all of my inconveniences of a certain type?" He lifted a brow which I mimicked, making him glare at me. "Now, back to the issue at hand. What are you going to do about Sophia's situation?"

"You told me to stay away from her. Have you changed your mind?"

"No. You aren't what a brother would pick for her."

I gestured with my chin below us to where Lucian's wife, Elaine, stood, talking with her older brother Winston. "Are you saying your lady's brothers would say you're the perfect match for her?"

"You're an asshole, Pierce."

"As are you, Morelli."

Lucian's face grew hard.

"I want that fucker handled."

"Did you forget I don't take orders from you?"

"You need to remember that our history will never supersede the fact she's my baby sister, and you fucked with her life."

"I had no intention of hurting her."

"Too fucking late for that."

His words felt like a direct blow to the gut. I'd screwed it up royally. My visit to Randolph may have added more fuel to Sophia's notorious reputation and ruined her career.

"He won't be a problem for her in the future."

"Meaning?"

I held his hard stare. "I'll take care of it. That is all you need to know."

✧ ✧ ✧

"I WANT IT set in motion as soon as possible," I relayed over the phone to my investigator and security leads, who were all on the line. "I want it airtight. Nothing will link back to her."

I paused as a discussion broke out about connecting my plans for Randolph to me.

Cutting them off, I said, "If and when that possibility arises, we will deal with it. Besides, I'm not the only player with grievances against him on the board. I can think of at least eight other suspects in addition to myself. So the concern isn't necessary."

After a few more moments, I hung up. I tucked my cell phone into my suit pocket, strolled into the ballroom, and immediately regretted it.

Sophia stood near the center of the room, wielding her power and completely oblivious to her effect on the people around her.

Why hadn't I gone with my instinct and left as soon as the dedication and speeches ended? It would have been safer considering the plans I'd set in motion.

Now here I was, ready to break the hand of the next fucker who touched her.

Even with the scandal surrounding her, she commanded attention like a flame gathered moths. Men and women circled around her, discussing something or the other, many skimming a hand over her arm or grazing her back while they spoke.

Behavior that was entirely out of line in my book. And from how Sophia gracefully adjusted her position in the groups, she'd also agree.

In gatherings like tonight's, social graces and pedigree took center stage. Sophia wore the label of the Morelli wild child. Still, she understood proper behavior in a formal setting.

And if I hadn't spent most of the evening with a fucking hard-on, I'd have laughed at the way the society assholes seemed to fall all over themselves for a moment of her time.

The prick beside her stared adoringly at her as if she were his sun, moon, and stars. He wouldn't know what to do with someone like her. Yes, he'd revere her and give her the gentle passion he'd expect for a woman of her station, but he'd leave her wanting and unfulfilled.

Sweet and soft weren't even in the vicinity of her cravings.

With me, she'd have no mercy whatsoever. I'd take her home, fuck her mouth, her cunt, her ass.

She'd scream and beg for more. I'd possess her in every way possible.

Sophia was strong and not prone to melancholy. Hell, she'd faced so many challenges and kept her head high.

But I'd never gotten in so deep with any woman, not even Maria. With her, I cared and enjoyed her, but never this gut-wrenching call to protect, to keep safe, to hold, to put her first as I did with Sophia.

Maybe that made me a cold-hearted bastard.

I'd better walk away before I ruined Sophia too.

Attraction or not, Lucian was right. I wasn't the right man for her.

I took in her smile one last time as she chatted with an older woman near her.

So fucking beautiful.

A man with a similar build to me and black hair approached her from behind. He slid his arm around her waist and then leaned into her neck as if to kiss her shoulder. She jerked in surprise, trying to pull away until she recognized the person. Her frown turned into laughter, and she turned toward him, lifted up on tiptoes to kiss his cheek.

Who the fuck was that asshole?

I clenched my fist as rage stormed through me.

Sophia Morelli belonged to me. Every part of her was mine.

Whoever he was, he had no rights to her.

Before I realized it, I'd weaved my way through the crowded ballroom.

Pushing through the group around her, I ordered, "I'd get your hands off her if you know what's best for you."

Sophia whirled around as the man with her dropped his hold but blocked my way to her with his body.

"Who are you to tell me what I can and cannot do with Sophia?" he asked.

I glared at him. "She's my woman. So I suggest you never touch her in such a fashion again."

The man glanced at Sophia, who stepped around him. A slight smile touched her full lips, and she shook her head.

"Justine, I'm fine. Mr. Pierce wants to speak to me about something. I'll see you for our meeting later this coming week."

Concern crossed over this Justine's features, but he consented and then moved away.

Sophia's attention shifted to me. "That's very caveman of you."

"You have no idea." I stepped toward her. "Who was that?"

"Why do you care?"

"You know I damn well care. Now answer the question."

"My agent."

Agent? Who the fuck had an agent that looked like a billionaire cover model?

Sophia, that was who.

I narrowed my gaze. "Are all agents that familiar with their clients? If I hadn't known firsthand otherwise, I'd say the two of you were lovers."

"Are you jealous?"

"Let's put it this way. I showed remarkable restraint."

A flash of something, possibly uneasiness or vulnerability, passed in her black eyes. "Didn't we agree not to see each other in or out of the club again?"

I ignored her question. There was no going

back now.

"You're mine, Sophia. I don't share."

"Are you staking your claim, Mr. Pierce?"

"And if I said I am?"

"Do you plan to make the point clear in the same fashion as before?" She stepped closer to me, setting a hand on my tuxedo jacket.

She smelled so damn good.

Was she accepting what I'd said?

I wrapped an arm around Sophia's hip and guided her toward the dance floor.

"Not here. Your family wouldn't appreciate a display in that manner. For now, this will have to do."

Turning her to face me, I offered her my hand.

"Think very carefully about what you're doing. Dancing with me here will mean something. This isn't the club, and this isn't a scene where once it's over, you walk away." She swallowed as if she were finding the courage to finish her words.

Before she could speak, I said, "There is a reason why I kept pushing you away, why I refused to pursue this outside the club."

"And that is?"

"You meant something to me from that first night. It touched me on a level I couldn't explain.

It scared me. What I felt wasn't rational."

"Don't say things like that. It confuses me. You said point blank what we had stayed within the club's walls."

"I was protecting you. What happened at the fashion show pushed the lines. Pursuing our dynamic outside of the club comes with a lot more consequences."

A crease formed between her brows as if she were about to argue, but instead, she moved closer to me and lifted her hand, pausing right before she slid her palm over mine. "With me, you'll get high-profile incidents, galas, nosy reporters, and maybe a scandal or two. That isolated life you enjoy so much won't exist anymore."

"I threatened your agent for touching you a few minutes ago in front of a whole ballroom of people. That is sure to have some repercussions." I closed my fingers around hers, bringing her body in close. "Well, in that case. I guess we make a great pair."

"I should warn you."

She lifted a well-defined brow. "Oh, another warning. Let me hear it."

I resisted kissing her, knowing I'd caused enough chatter for the evening.

"I plan to fuck you as soon as I punish you for

CLAIM

pulling that stunt at that asshole's penthouse."

"Not happening." Then she quickly amended. "To the punishment part."

"Why is that?"

"You administer punishment at the time of the offense, not whenever you feel like it. Rules are rules."

I couldn't help but smile at her. "You most definitely are a brat."

"Don't say I didn't warn you." She glanced to her side and then up at me. "Want to get out of here and give everyone more gossip?"

"About that. We will need to discuss—"

"How dare you." An angry voice boomed behind me, making me stiffen.

Sophia and I stopped dancing and turned. There before us stood Harold Williams, Maria's brother. I couldn't blame him for the hate he directed toward me.

He'd aged in the last year and a half, looking closer to forty than his actual age of thirty. Maybe the grief of losing Maria or the years of drinking had taken its toll on him. But whatever it was, all I saw facing me right now was pure unadulterated hate.

I'd face it. I deserved it. I'd failed Maria. I hadn't seen the signs of her depression, her obsession with making me love her, and in the end, it cost her everything.

"Williams," I inclined my head, knowing the last thing he planned to do was keep up social graces.

"I cannot believe you would flaunt your next victim in front of all of New York society. And I doubt anyone will say a fucking word when she dies, just like no one gave a damn about my sister."

CHAPTER SIXTEEN
Sophia

I STARED IN complete dismay at the man before me.

So this was Damon's deceased submissive's brother. And he actually believed Damon killed her, even though all evidence showed otherwise.

Harold looked around him and then said in a louder voice. "This man is responsible for my sister Maria's death, and no one cared. Will you care when she dies?"

From the periphery, I noticed my family moving in our direction, which meant I'd better get this situation under control.

"Who's Maria?" I asked, even though I knew. "Perhaps if you explained things, I'd understand your anger better."

I wanted to see what he'd say. How far he'd push it. He'd already created the scene. Maybe if I drew his attention to me, I could calm the situation down.

"My sister." Harold's manic blue eyes bore into mine, and then he pointed at Damon. "And this man killed her."

Gasps came from around us, and the bleakness shadowing Damon's face crushed me. An incident like this was the last thing he'd want to happen in public, a scene where emotions skewed the truth.

My heart ached for Harold too.

He'd lost his sister, and I could only imagine how he felt.

No matter how strained things became with my family, I couldn't bear to think of how I'd handle losing a single one of them.

Slowly I step between Harold and Damon, drawing Harold's focus back to me. "I'm so sorry for your loss. I can see how much you loved her and miss her. But you must realize this isn't how to remember her."

"Anything is better than forgetting." He scrubbed a hand down his face, resignation etched all over it. "That's what he wants to do. He wants to forget she ever existed."

Damon remained quiet, stoically standing behind me. Why wouldn't he defend himself? He told me about the regret he carried. He mourned her too.

Why wouldn't he tell Harold that he blamed himself for the choice Maria made with her life?

Tears burned the back of my throat as I realized Damon believed he deserved Harold's wrath and the humiliation of this confrontation in front of everyone.

Oh. No. He would not carry that on his shoulders.

The hell with that bullshit.

If he wouldn't defend himself, I'd do it.

"Why do you keep blaming Damon for her death? As I understand it, she took her own life. It's tragic, but it's not—"

"It was murder," Harold shouted, cutting me off. "Maybe once he takes his second victim, people will finally accept the truth about him."

I'd had enough of this. Harold's pain had destroyed his ability to think straight, and now, the entire ballroom seemed invested in this interaction involving the three of us.

Plus, the anger radiating through the glares Father directed in our direction meant I only garnered a few more minutes before he interjected himself in this situation.

"Enough with this tirade." I gestured to the exit. "You've said your peace and caused an unnecessary scene. It's time for you to leave."

"My sister loved him until the end. Don't follow in her footsteps." He shook his head and strode in the direction of the doors.

The room remained silent for a few seconds. Then the roar returned to its previous state.

I turned my head to ask Damon if he was ready to leave, but he wasn't behind me.

Where had he gone?

Lucian and Elaine approached me.

Lucian offered me his free elbow and said, "Have you finally come to your senses and realized someone like him isn't good for you?"

"Is there anyone good enough for her?" Elaine asked him as she tucked a stray blonde hair behind her ear.

Lucian shot her a sideways glare and then focused back on me. "I don't want Sophia involved in the shit that haunts him."

"We have just as many ghosts in our closets," I interjected and then added. "Cleansing our family would require an exorcism."

"You don't need to add Pierce's issues onto your shoulders. Don't you think you have enough to handle, considering the shit you're wading through with the designer? Something that I'll remind you started because of Pierce's interference."

"Didn't Damon prove that I mean something to him tonight?" I asked.

"It will take more to impress me than nearly causing a brawl in the middle of a ballroom out of jealousy."

I rolled my eyes. "You said he wasn't the type for grand gestures. He proved you wrong. There is more to us than jealousy."

Lucian clenched his jaw, and at that exact moment, Elaine lifted her face, gave him a pointed stare, and said, "Tell her what you told me. Then she will understand your reservation about her relationship."

"If she listened to anything I said, none of this would have happened in the first place."

"Listening to you and having you make my choices for me are two different things. It's my life." I resisted the urge to stomp on his foot for being an overbearing ass. "Just spill it, and we can move on."

Lucian shifted his annoyed attention from Elaine to me. "The timeline of events that led up to his sub's death doesn't add up. The way Maria's brother described her and what Pierce knew about her made it seem as if they were talking about two different people. That is why Pierce blames himself. It is a mystery he will never stop wanting to solve. Are you sure you want to live with that hanging over your head?"

"As long as Damon understands, I am not her, and I am not like her. Then, we are fine. I'm not like anyone. I'm especially not the type of daughter Bryant and Sarah Morelli believe I should be."

We walked to the back of the building in the direction of an elaborate garden.

"You aren't going to take my advice no matter what I say, are you?"

"I'm the female version of you. Haven't you figured it out? We, the black sheep of the family, have to stick together."

Lucian tsk'd, "You have no idea how wrong you are."

"Why don't you explain it then, all-knowing Lucian Morelli."

A snort escaped Elaine's lips, which caused mine to twitch for a moment. Only Elaine and I got away with making light of situations around hard-nosed Lucian without annoying him too much.

Not missing a beat, he released a suffering sigh and shook his head. "You feel pain, Sophia. Whereas I don't. I'm a cold-blooded bastard."

I rolled my eyes, glancing at Elaine, who

pursed her lips, trying to hold in a laugh.

Lucian leaned down toward Elaine's ear. "I'm glad you find me amusing. Maybe you won't later."

"Maybe, I will." She gave him a sweet smile, and he shook his head as his own lips quirked up at the sides.

Correction, it was with Elaine he truly showed a softer side. Lucian rarely joked and never laughed before Elaine. He tolerated my nonsense, but for his wife, there was another side to him only she saw.

When we reached the end doors to the garden, Lucian released my arm and turned the knob. "He went into the greenhouse."

"You confuse the hell out of me." I frowned at him. "Why are you helping me if you want me away from him?"

"You made your decision the second you realized he left the room. At least you won't get into any more trouble if I know where you are tonight. Try not to let the papz get shots of your antics, hmm."

"Thanks. I think." I gave Lucian the side eye as he pushed me out into the cool air and promptly closed the door in my face.

Well, okay then.

Turning, I made my way to the greenhouse.

It stood separate from the central event building, with tinted glass on all sides and greenery planted around the base. Solar panels constructed most of the east and west-facing roof angles, and glass encompassed all other parts.

This definitely wasn't the typical style of structure found in the middle of New York City. The whole area was an oasis for the occupants who lived or worked in the vicinity.

I approached the greenhouse and readied to shift the sliding door but hesitated.

An uncomfortable sensation crept into my stomach, making me wonder if coming here was the right idea after all.

Would he turn me away? Could I handle it if he'd changed his mind about us once again? This hot and cold shit had to stop.

Fuck it.

No time for second-guessing myself. Besides, once I decided on a course of action, I never faltered.

I tugged the lever, unlatched the lock, and moved inside the building. I scanned the area as the rich scent of soil and plant life assaulted my senses, and a thick layer of balmy humidity cascaded over my skin.

Tucked behind the aisles of freshly budding potted flowers, I spotted Damon sitting hunched over with his arms propped on his knees and his hands gripping his head.

He'd tossed his tux jacket and bow tie somewhere and rolled his shirtsleeves up to the elbows. An aura of loneliness and resignation flowed around him, giving me the urge to wrap him in my arms.

As if sensing me, he lifted his head.

The bleakness in his green eyes had me swallowing the lump in my throat. It was as if he believed he deserved to be alone, not that he wanted to be alone.

The longing, the need between us, so thick, so visceral. Until I met this man, I'd never felt this type of draw to anyone. I wanted to soothe him, heal him, please him, and give him comfort. It was as if something deep in me craved this with every fiber of my being.

The way he stared at me broke my heart. It was as if he reached for me. He knew I'd break from the barest pass of his touch.

If only he understood how much I needed his hands on me.

I locked the door behind me and slowly made my way closer to him.

"What are you doing here, Sophia?" His voice sounded more like he cautioned me to keep my distance than ask a question.

"I came to find you."

"Why?"

"That's a dumb question."

"I'm not in the mood for your attitude right now." The way his voice deepened sent a flutter deep inside my core, and arousal hummed in my blood.

"What attitude? This is my base setting, or haven't you realized this by now?"

A creased formed between his brows for a fraction of a second before he schooled it away. "Coming in here was a bad idea."

"Why?"

"Because I'm not good for you. Stay away from me, Sophia." The hard edge of his order pushed against every urge inside me to defy him.

"Or what?"

"You may become my next victim. Are you sure you want to risk it?" He held my gaze. "I'm a murderer, didn't you hear? I'm responsible for Maria's death. It would be best if you walked away while you had the chance."

"You should know by now that I don't listen very well. I tend to do the opposite of what everyone tells me. So my answer to your question is. I'll take my chances."

He adjusted his position on the bench, his focus on me now almost menacing. "Sophia, you don't have a clue as to what you are getting into with me."

"Why don't you elaborate." I strolled closer to him, his green eyes narrowing with each step I took.

The lust that covered his face now told me the chivalrous side of him had lost the war within himself.

In the back of my mind, a little warning told me to stop and not be reckless. To hell with that voice. I wanted this man, and for once, I'd do something I was accused of doing.

"Last warning. The second my hands touch you, you've made your decision."

I licked my lips. "What decision is that?"

"To accept my claim. In public and private. That means in and out of the club."

"So that show in the ballroom before we danced, wasn't you deciding for me?"

"I conveyed my intentions."

"I see, and then you walked away." I let my annoyance show in my tone. "It isn't me that needs to make a solid decision, Mr. Pierce. You need to figure out where the fuck you stand."

"I know exactly where I stand, Miss Morelli." He rose to his feet, his height a towering presence with me only a few steps away.

My skin burned for his touch, and the throbbing deep inside me grew to a painful level.

Holding his heated gaze, I asked, "And where exactly is that?"

"Right here." He captured my throat in an unyielding hold and moved in until the front of his body brushed against mine. "You belong to me now."

My nipples pebbled, and desire pooled between my legs. "You think so."

"I know so. I'm claiming you everywhere."

"Only where I let you." I clutched his shoulders as my eyes fluttered closed from the exquisite feel of his fingers flexing on my skin.

"There is no 'let.' I warned you what would happen the moment I touched you. I am your Dom. I've claimed your body, your mind, your soul."

His words stirred something deep inside me. Was it fear or comfort?

Fuck I had no idea.

"What does that mean?"

"I will take care of you, I will pleasure you,

and I will punish you. You're my submissive from this point forward."

I looked into his heated eyes. "You mean until this fire between us burns out. Then it will end."

"Oh, this isn't going to end. I'm keeping you. And we both know this fire, as you put it, will only grow more intense. It will turn into an inferno that nothing can put out."

CHAPTER SEVENTEEN

Damon

"You can't keep me unless I allow it." The feel of Sophia's pulse under my fingers shot a surge of lust straight to my cock.

"You'll allow it," I said to Sophia as I stared into her midnight eyes.

"What makes you so sure?"

I wanted to punish her, make her cry, bask in her pain for not listening to me, for not running away, for pushing and pushing when I told her I was not the one for her, not the man she should ever allow to claim her.

Bringing my face a fraction from hers, I stated, "You felt it from the first moment our eyes connected. It's only grown more intense. This thing between us is inevitable. Doing the right thing is no longer an option."

I'd never lie to myself and say I hadn't loved every second of her defending me. She'd masterfully turned the situation on Williams, making it very clear to all who listened that he was a grief-stricken brother who couldn't accept the truth of his sister's death.

But it also put her in the middle of another scandal. That was all she needed.

I guessed she'd survive this one as she had the others.

And then there was Lucian. He'd threaten to kill me. It's exactly what I'd do if I were in his position, knowing the shit I did about myself.

My reputation and my preferences weren't hidden.

And then there was Bryant Morelli and the other Morelli brothers. By now, they had every piece of information on me, from my birth records to what I ate for breakfast. Well, what I made available to the public.

They'd want my head on a platter.

"The right thing is overrated. It's more fun to break the rules."

I planned to defile this woman in every way possible.

Coasting my mouth across hers, I brushed her lips and bit down hard enough to cause a sting and make her gasp without breaking the skin.

"You are mine now. I'm a possessive fucking bastard, My Sophia. You're going to learn what that means in great detail."

"I—is that a threat?" She lifted a brow in a challenge, but the unsteady way she asked and the jumping of her heartbeat under my fingers told me her question was all bravado.

"You'll have to find out and see." Then, taking one of her wrists in my free hand, I pinned it to her back and crashed my mouth over hers.

She tasted of champagne and cinnamon candy, a sweet, decadent blend only she could make me want to get my fill of.

I wanted all of her, to consume her, to infiltrate every part of her, to possess her.

I only hoped these very things about me wouldn't eventually make her run away. I had no doubt it would, but for now, I'd delight in it and indulge to my heart's content.

Her fingers threaded into my hair, and she scored her nails against my scalp sending shivers and desire throughout my body.

The need to fuck her roared inside me. This woman who kept pushing, who refused to listen. The brat who needed to poke and prod until she received the reaction she craved.

I walked her backward until she was pinned to a butcher block table. A whimper escaped her throat as I nipped her sensitive bottom lip, and she broke the kiss.

Passion and hunger laced her dark eyes. "What was that for?"

"Sophia, it's time you understood what you've gotten yourself into."

Ignoring the confusion etched on her features, I turned her and bent her over the table. I pulled my tie from my pocket and wrapped it around her wrists, making sure to bind her so she wouldn't lose circulation and keep her from finding a way to free herself.

"Are you crazy? This place is made of glass."

"You wanted me. Now you have me. That means I get to fuck you and punish you, any damn place I please." I cupped her plump ass, and she immediately pushed into my touch. "From your response, you don't seem so opposed to the idea."

"It's because I'm sex-deprived, nothing more."

"Let me guess. Ever since my cock claimed your cunt, your toys don't seem to make the cut." The thought of her using anything on her pussy without my permission sent a pang of irritation through me.

"You didn't have a claim on me, so why do you care?"

I gripped her hair, jerking her head back. "I

claimed that cunt the second I took your virginity. You're mine. And you made it even more official when you walked in here tonight. You are mine, Sophia Morelli. This was your choice. Time to get fucking used to it."

Releasing her, I pushed her forward until the side of her face pressed to the table.

"Instead of worrying about the window, you may want to consider someone walking in on us." I settled my hand over her bound ones and kicked her legs apart before I lifted her dress to expose her barely-there thong.

God, I couldn't wait to fuck that ass of hers, to make her beg to come, to make her cry as I pounded into her.

She deserved it for not listening and not letting me do the right thing.

"I locked the door when I came in."

"Why?" I asked right before I brought my hand down hard.

"Fuck," she cried out. "Are you out of your mind?"

Ignoring her, I smacked her ass again and commanded, "Answer my question."

"You know why." She lifted into the strike of my palm, wanting more of the sting against her skin.

"Say it." My thumb slid along the damp fabric of her thong until it reached her swollen clit and then circled.

She widened her legs and shifted side to side, trying to get the exact friction she craved.

"More," she sobbed, tears streaming from her eyes. "Please."

"I can do this all night long and never let you come."

She clenched her teeth and said, "Because I knew you'd fuck me once you stopped living in your head and realized I could handle anything you threw my way."

I stared at her tear-streaked, flushed face as something, unlike anything I'd ever experienced locked into place inside me. This woman pushed and pushed until I had no defenses left.

Now if only disaster wasn't looming in the distance.

Pushing the thought back, I refocused on the jewel before me.

I leaned forward and whispered to her, "I thought you were worried about someone seeing us through the windows. Or was that an act?"

"I wasn't thinking about the windows when I came in here. Stop talking." She turned her head to stare into my eyes. "I need more."

Even bound and at my mercy, the defiance of this woman made no fucking sense. She was everything that I'd never found attractive in others. Except with her, I only wanted to gain that submission from the defiant brat she loved to play.

And that submission was oh so beautiful, full of tears, surrender, and abandoned pleasure.

"More, what?"

"I don't care anymore. I need to come."

I nipped her lower lip and pulled back. "In that case, let me resume my original objective."

Her eyes narrowed as she realized what I had planned, and then she released a gasp, followed by a moan after I resumed spanking the globes of her ass.

I covered every inch of it in a rosy glow, and all I heard was a stream of nonsensical begging from her lips.

"Please, Damon. Please." The beautiful way her mascara smudged down her cheeks with her tears had me ready to come in my pants.

"You want to come. I'll let you come. But from now on, it's only with my permission." I freed my cock from my pants and tugged her underwear down. "I claim every one of your orgasms from this point on. Is that understood?"

I positioned the head of my cock at her soaked entrance.

She whimpered and moaned, trying to leverage against the table's edge. "Fuck me already."

"Answer my question, and then you'll get what you want," I said, holding her still with my weight along her back. "As I said before, I can wait all night until I get my answer."

Sliding a hand under her, I tugged her back, notching myself into her, but going no further. "We both know I can win any sexual challenge. Or do you need me to remind you of our first night together?"

"You know the answers to all the questions, so why do you need to hear me say them?"

"Because I'm your Dom, and you do as I say." I pushed in a little more, feeling her flex around my cock, giving it a wicked squeeze. "Who owns every one of your orgasms, Sophia?"

"You do," she whispered.

"Have you made yourself come since that day at the fashion show?"

She shook her head. "No."

"Why not?"

"I don't know." A mewled moan tore through her as I pushed in a fraction more.

"I believe you do know."

"Damon, please. I'm dying here."

"Then answer the question truthfully."

She sighed in resignation. "Because I wanted you to give it to me. I should hate you for making me want you like this."

"But you don't."

"But I don't."

"Good to know." I slammed into her.

Her back bowed, and she gasped aloud, "Finally."

"Always the brat." I took hold of her bound hands and set a relentless pace, fucking into her like a man possessed.

Her delicious pussy quivered and flexed with each pass of my pistoning cock. And I couldn't get enough.

The table jostled with each of my thrusts, sending planters, bottles, and gardening tools to the ground.

She arched and then looked over her shoulder, pleading with her eyes and words, "More, please more."

I rolled my hips, hitting the sensitive spot deep inside her, and in the next second, she detonated, clamping down in rhythmic spasms and then tightened like a brutal fist.

Something primal filled me, and my pace

grew harder and more demanding.

I reached forward and cupped her throat as my own orgasm shot through me.

"You're mine now, Sophia Morelli. Admit it."

"Yes, I'm yours," she responded as she continued to ride out her release.

"There is no escape for you now."

CHAPTER EIGHTEEN

Sophia

"I TOLD YOU to listen, but you never do."

"I followed your exact orders. Nothing I ever do pleases you. I'll never be good enough."

"You wouldn't know how to please me if someone gave you a step-by-step instruction manual. You're useless, Sarah."

Oh God, they're shouting again.

I wished I lived somewhere else. Anywhere else was better than here. I hated this place.

A shiver slid down my spine, and the cold seeped into my skin, chilling me to the bone. I wrapped my blanket around my shoulders tighter in a failed effort to find some warmth.

The way my body shook wasn't from the fever caused by the virus coursing through my body but the fear of what would happen once the yelling came in this direction of the house.

Mom always ran in this direction in hopes of escaping Father. Sometimes, he left her alone, but most of the time, he followed.

No, that wasn't the right word for what he enjoyed doing to her.

He chased her, stalked her, cornered her. He loved to trap her like an animal and make her feel like she had nowhere to run.

And if she somehow hid well enough and one of us children crossed his path, we'd suffer the consequences. The few times I managed to land in his sights were times I'd never want to relive.

I had to be ready in case Father's anger turned on me.

Pushing back my covers, I found my slippers, slid them on my feet, and then grabbed my robe, shrugging it on and tying my belt tight.

I searched the room for the best spot to disappear.

Only the driver and a few household staff knew I had arrived home early. If all else failed, I could sneak into one of my brothers' rooms.

Oh, why couldn't the school nurse have had mercy on me and let me stay in class for a few more hours? But, instead, she'd called the family driver to pick me up.

No matter how much I begged, telling her that the kids in my class were the ones who gave me the bug in the first place, so I was fine staying in school, she insisted I had to go home.

Now here I was, in the middle of the chaos of my parents.

My lips trembled as I squeezed my arms around my body.

I wanted my brothers.

They would protect me. They always protected me. But they were all at school, and I hadn't felt safe ever since they left.

A girl should feel safe in her home, but not me.

Sophia Donatella Morelli had no such luxury in this house full of secrets everyone pretended never existed. I wasn't blind. I saw things. I knew things.

So many lies, so many half-truths. And a father who couldn't forget his past, so he covered it with anger and alcohol.

A blood-curdling scream reached my ear, followed by a sharp thud, making me cringe. My body shook as tears filled my eyes.

Slowly a low whimper came through the wall my bedroom shared with the library. Then came the sounds of flesh on flesh and uncontrollable sobs.

Mom.

Father had dragged her in there and now was hurting her again. It wouldn't matter if Mom talked back or remained utterly stoic. He'd find some excuse to take out his rage on her.

He believed if he handled things behind closed doors, people wouldn't know.

Everyone knew. His friends. His business partners. His social circle. And most assuredly, his household staff.

They never spoke about it to his face, only behind his back.

Without thought, I found a spot in the far corner of my closet, under my winter clothes, and curled into a ball, hoping no one would know I was there. Maybe Father wouldn't figure out I was home if I stayed quiet.

Whenever Lucian was around, he'd storm in and find some way to protect our mother, even if it meant suffering our father's wrath.

I so wished I had his strength to fight back. But then again, the few times I'd gotten in the way... No, I shook the thought from my mind.

Suddenly, everything grew quiet, and a lump formed in the pit of my stomach.

Oh God, what could he have done?

Gingerly, I crept out from under my clothes and trekked to the door connecting my bedroom and the library. It was more of a sliding panel, and most people had no idea it existed. I only knew of it because Lucian had shown it to me when I was seven, and I used it as a fun way to escape from the family. It was my special secret with my big brother.

Moving past the large dressing table opposite my bed, I touched the latch holding the panel closed, and pulled it down as quietly as possible.

Then I shimmied the wall a crack open when

strange noises erupted from the room. These were sounds I'd heard before, ones that frightened me.

I shouldn't look. It was better. I turned around and pretended I wasn't there.

Heart drumming in my chest, I peeked through the opening, hating everything I saw.

No. No. No.

"Sophia, wake up."

I gasped in shallow breaths, unable to comprehend where I was, as fear overwhelmed my body.

"Oh God, oh God, oh God." I shoved at the hands holding me.

"Sophia. It's Damon. You're safe. I'm here. I won't let anyone hurt you."

"No, no, no. It's not okay. It's not safe."

"Open your eyes and look at me."

The command had me jolting, and slowly, realization crept in.

It was the dream. That fucking dream.

Sweat covered every inch of my body, and the rawness of my throat told me I'd screamed my terror.

Lifting my lashes, I stared up at Damon through tear-filled eyes. The concern on his face had my heart clenching. I couldn't remember a time when anyone held me after a nightmare.

I'd never screamed in all the times I'd relived this memory. I kept quiet every time, no matter the confusion, shock, or horror of seeing my parents with that third person.

In my memories, I'd closed the panel, hidden away again until the noises stopped. Then, I'd kept anyone from knowing I'd arrived home early and pretended everything was normal, going as far as to change back into my school clothes.

It wasn't until later in the evening that I'd let Mom notice that I'd caught an illness. And as usual, she'd handed me off to the live-in nanny to care for me since she had to attend an event.

A sick child was no reason to cancel any social engagement.

Damon reached over to the bedside table, turned on the lamp, and grabbed a glass of water before bringing it to my lips. "Drink this."

The cool liquid eased the discomfort in my throat, and I released a sigh. "Thank you for waking me."

"You were panicking in absolute terror. It took shouting in your face to wake you up." His arms tighten around me. "Do you have nightmares like this often?"

"Once in a while, but nothing like this. I've never cried out or woken anyone before."

"Want to talk about it?"

Talk about it. Umm no.

The dream made no sense, especially since the ending wasn't how it usually went. But why couldn't I remember what happened in the room this time?

I shook my head. "No, I can't even explain it to myself. I'm not sure how I would be able to tell you."

Setting the glass back on the side table, he tilted my chin. "Tell me what you remember."

His serious gaze and the worry etched there had my heartbeat accelerating. He was all in with this thing we'd started tonight in the greenhouse.

"I can't put it into comprehensible words for myself. So how am I going to tell you?" I cup his cheek, giving him a slight smile. "It's over now. I'm okay. You took care of me."

The crease between his brows said I'd far from convinced him that I'd spoken the truth. Instead of saying something as I'd expected, he pressed a button on a controller near his side of the headboard, and the curtains drew open to reveal a breathtaking one-eighty-degree view of the New York City skyline at night. Then he landed back, pulling me against him.

After we remained quiet for a few minutes, he

asked, "Are you not telling me because of what Williams said about me? Did I cause the nightmare?"

"Of course not." I turned to face him, resting my arms on his bare chest. "The dream had nothing to do with you."

But now that he'd brought it up—nope, this wasn't the time to go there. My emotions were a hot mess, and I wasn't thinking straight.

I dropped my head down and studied the buildings in the cityscape.

"Oh no, you don't." He threaded his fingers in my hair, tugging my head up. "I saw that look. What just passed through that beautiful mind of yours?"

Could I go there? And would knowing make things easier?

Yes, I needed to know. I had to ask.

Ever since I met Damon, I felt the heavy presence of the woman who'd once occupied the place I did now. I refused to be the third person in anyone's relationship. My mother may have been fine with those terms, but the hell if I was.

Dead or not, her specter haunted what Damon and I had. He'd made too many decisions about us based on the tragedy of her death.

Now or never, Sophia.

"I want to know about Maria. I want to know your side, all of it."

He stiffened. His eyes darkened to almost a deep emerald, and then he nodded. He freed his grip on my hair and lifted his arm, and I settled more comfortably along his body.

"It's true. I killed her."

Without thought, I sat up and said, "Bullshit. She took her own life. That does not make you her killer."

"So fierce to defend me, even from me."

I scowled at him. "I'm giving you a reality check."

"Is that what you're calling it?" He shook his head and then jerked me back against him. "You don't even have a clue as to the type of man who's claimed you. Listen to the tale and then decide."

"Decide what exactly?"

"Whether or not you've bound yourself to the villain of the story."

The way he'd spoken, he truly believed he was responsible for Maria's death.

"Tell me, and then I'll make the call. I know villains firsthand. In some senses, I am one."

His arms tightened around me. "Oh, My Sophia, that incident at the prick designer's place was child's play. Maybe one day, I'll divulge some of the antics Lucian and I engaged in during our younger years."

"First, I want to hear about Maria."

"I guess there is no diverting you from a mission."

"Nope."

He released a deep breath and started talking, "My dynamic with Maria wasn't a basic level of power exchange, but absolute power exchange."

He paused, waiting for me to ask questions, but I remained quiet.

"She devoted herself completely to me and relied on me for everything. Love wasn't a factor in our relationship. It went along the lines of ownership. She wanted me to control every aspect of her life. She expected it, craved it. She'd flounder when I couldn't provide that extreme level of control. I was responsible for her twenty-four hours a day, seven days a week."

A pang of jealousy coursed through me, knowing he'd been with someone who'd been at his beck and call for anything he wanted.

I understood some women needed that release from making any decisions. They felt safer having someone protect them, make all their decisions, and keep them as pets or slaves. But that wasn't me. I could never be someone like that. My DNA made me a brat and mouthy by nature.

I loved the sparring game of back and forth and skating the line of going too far. The thought of being under anyone's thumb to that level pushed every one of my buttons to run.

If this was what he'd had, I'd never match up. Could he live with what came with me long-term?

"I know what you are thinking." I opened my mouth, ready to argue, but he commanded, "Stop. Listen to the rest of it."

"Yes, sir."

"Very funny," he muttered before continuing. "I enjoyed the control, I loved her submission, but I knew I wasn't the right Dom for her. The level of devotion she needed wasn't something I had the ability to give her. I enjoy complete submission. I live for it. However, I do not want to live it at every moment of every day. She deserved someone better than me.

"I explained it to her, and she said she understood, but she hadn't. And it was my fault for continuing our dynamic even after I realized we weren't a good fit for each other. Our scenes together should tell you how intense I am."

Yeah, he overwhelmed the senses and made a girl feel like she was the only woman on earth.

"In Maria's mind, she believed my passion for

her was love, and all she had to do was convince me of what I felt. She couldn't separate the physical aspect of our lives from the emotional.

"I broke it off when I realized she still believed we had a future together. I'd even gone as far as to offer to introduce her to Doms who were better suited for her, but she refused and begged me to stay with her. Then she threatened me and anyone else I took as a submissive. In her eyes, she devoted herself to me, and I threw her away. My intensity and possessive nature brought her to the point where she couldn't accept we were over. Finally, when she realized none of her tactics would get me to budge on my decision, she stormed out of my old penthouse, saying she wouldn't go on without me."

"You thought it was another ploy to get you to change your mind."

"I failed her. It was my duty to take care of her, meet her needs, and keep her safe. Her last words were a cry for help, and I let her walk out the door. The next morning, her brother called with the news. I might as well have killed her." He wiped a hand across his face as he gazed at his intricately designed ceiling. "Didn't I tell you I was the villain?"

He had to be kidding me.

"Mr. Pierce, you're neither the hero of the story nor the villain." Pushing up to sitting, I climbed over to straddle him and leaned down.

Surprise and confusion played over his face for a second before he gripped my hips in a firm hold. "Is that right? Want to explain this with your Morelli logic?"

"Did you or didn't you tell her that you weren't right for her?"

"You heard my story, so you know the answers."

Pressing my palms to his bare chest, I retorted, "I don't think you seem to understand them very well."

"I understand completely. I know my role as a Dom. I refuse to make the same mistakes with you that I made with her."

"Do I look fragile to you?" I asked, bringing my face down until we were nose to nose and letting him see my annoyance. "I am not her. You will never put me in the same category as her again."

"Is that right?"

"Yes."

Before I knew what he planned, he flipped me onto my back, pinning my arms above my head, and loomed over me. The raw masculine beauty of him had my blood heating and wet heat pooling between my legs. His wicked gleam told me he knew how my body reacted to him. And from the way his cock lay hard and heavy between us, he felt the same way about me.

He wedged his thighs between mine, spreading my knees apart. "Haven't you figured it out? You're in a category of your own."

"Which is?" I tried to lift my hips, desperate for the feel of him inside of me, but he stayed out of reach.

"Claimed."

"I don't buy that. You've had submissives before. We just discussed Maria."

He slammed into me, making me cry out.

"You're not Maria. Didn't you say that? And it's one thousand percent true." He pulled out and thrust back in just as hard, and the pleasure-filled pain brought tears to my eyes. "I've never claimed a woman. You're the first, and you have no fucking idea what that means."

"Tell me then."

I tugged at my arms, needing to touch him, but his fingers tightened on my wrists as his other hand grabbed my leg, positioning it over his shoulder.

He pumped in and out, working me, driving

my desire higher, making me orgasm over and over.

And right when I was ready to beg him to stop making me come, he pushed us over the crest and said, "Claiming you means you're fucking mine, Sophia. I will use any means necessary to protect you. I'm not letting you go. I can't. This was why Lucian didn't want us together. There is no escape for you now."

CHAPTER NINETEEN

Damon

A LITTLE BEFORE seven in the morning, I leaned against my wraparound balcony on my penthouse terrace, drinking a cup of coffee.

I'd spent most of the night lost in Sophia. The woman pushed every one of my buttons, and I couldn't get enough of her. The need to see the fire in her eyes, to punish her, to watch her cry, to fuck her until she begged me to let her sleep burned in my blood.

It was like nothing I'd experienced before. Putting words to the emotions, desires, and drive to protect her meant making her vulnerable.

What if I pushed her into the same state Maria had fallen into?

I shook the thought from my head. Sophia's strength went beyond anyone I'd ever met. She'd walk away with her head held high before she'd let anyone destroy her. Hell, she'd punch someone in the face on her way out.

No matter how much I wished otherwise, the guilt over Maria's death would forever stay locked away in the back of my mind. I'd never forget the shock and numbness I'd felt. Williams had raged at me, blamed me for bringing her into the life, for forcing her to my wicked ways.

I hadn't defended myself. I never revealed the truth about his sister and the fact she'd been a submissive to other Doms long before we'd ever gotten together. Williams wouldn't have believed me even if I'd tried. He grieved out of love for a lost sister. What I felt was only guilt.

Maybe if I'd tried harder, I could have loved her.

Who the fuck was I kidding? I'd had no heart to give a woman. The concepts of physical needs and protection were ingrained into me but love never sat on the list.

I was so much like the building I created, structured and soulless.

Until I met Sophia.

What the ever-loving fuck had I gotten myself into? The woman made me feel. For her, I found myself doing things I'd never considered before in my life.

First, the incident in the common room at the club and then last night in the ballroom.

The thought of anyone else touching her, being with her, made me murderous.

She was mine. Mine to fuck, mine to punish, mine to watch shed those beautiful tears.

Until her, no one stood up for me or sought to defend me.

Only an idiot wouldn't fall for a woman like that. So I'd do everything in my power to shield her from the Randolphs of the world. I'd rid the earth of them without a second thought.

Randolph would learn soon enough the consequences of ignoring my warning. Lucian took care of things his way. I handled things more cleanly. Well, my way left less chance of evidence.

Although, the method Lucian wanted me to use to end the situation had its merits too. And technically, the original idea came from me.

Not so long ago, Lucian had used one of my construction sites to dispose of a celebrity, rockstar, or something who'd interfered in his relationship with Elaine.

No matter, Randolph wouldn't trouble Sophia or any other innocent again.

Was this the type of devotion Maria craved from me? A pang of guilt hit me. It would never have been possible. I never felt for her what roars through my blood for Sophia.

Fuck, I'd send myself on a head trip.

Downing my coffee, I turned to set my cup on a nearby table. That was when my cell phone rang with an incoming call.

Reading the display, I groaned inside and picked up. "This better be important, Morelli. Especially since it isn't even seven in the morning, so spit it out."

"If you hurt her, I'll make your life a living hell."

"You made that threat already. Want to come up with a new one?"

"She's my sister. Do you expect me to condone what you're doing with her?"

"For a sadist kink club owner, you play the pearl-clutching church lady very well." I set an arm against the railing. "Does your wife know this side of your nature?"

"I should have taken care of you years ago."

"Probably." I shrugged, even knowing he couldn't see me. "Then again, you needed someone in your life who wasn't scared of you. I was the only one who qualified."

"You don't deserve her."

"She's an adult and makes her own decisions. Besides, if you're so against us being together, why did you direct her to the greenhouse?"

"She would have found you eventually. Nothing deters her once she puts her mind to something. I only kept her from causing another incident looking for you."

I glanced toward the doors on the far side of the terrace connecting to my bedroom, where Sophia still slept. "Are you so sure about this? There is a chance being with me got her into trouble last night."

He ignored my question and focused on the latter part of my statement, "Speaking of trouble. How are you handling the situation you created for Sophia with media outlets and tabloids? The fucker has put her through enough. I want him out of her life."

"I have things in motion. She's mine to protect." I had no doubt Lucian heard the underlying context in my words.

"So it's like that, is it?"

"Yes."

"Good to know. One last question for you."

"I'm listening."

"Do you regret not letting me handle the brother after everything went down? You could have avoided the drama of last night."

"It depends on the day. At the moment, no. I'm in a better place than he is." I lifted my gaze to see Sophia standing in the doorway between the living room and the balcony terrace.

She'd freshened up, with her face bare of makeup, wearing her hair in a knot atop her head, and donning one of my dress shirts. The material engulfed her petite frame, looking more like an oversized dress as it skimmed the bottom of her knees.

This was the unguarded Sophia Morelli. How long would she last before the walls slid back up?

And how much of my conversation had she heard? I guessed I'd find out soon enough.

"Are we done, Morelli?" I asked, wanting to end the call.

"We're done. Remember my warning, Pierce."

"Fuck off." I hung up the phone as Sophia lifted a brow.

"Lucian, I take it?" She moved in my direction. "You two have an interesting relationship."

"It is what it is."

"Most people don't talk to him the way you do."

"The same can be said in reverse."

A crease formed between her brows as she studied me. "Are you so much like him?"

"Yes and no. He's more in your face. I take a more low-key approach."

"Which of you is more…ummm." She tapped her lip.

"Unhinged, you mean? I'll give it to your brother. But I may give him a run for his money if it came to you."

Something flared in her dark eyes. Was it surprise or something else?

"Then I guess I shouldn't call on this architect I know to help me escape this mansion in the sky. He is good at helping me get out of tight situations."

"It's too late for that. You're trapped, or didn't I make it clear enough to you." I grabbed her hips as she neared, drawing her against me.

"Let me remind you that I'm only here as long as I want to be."

"And we both know you're not going to leave any time in the foreseeable future."

She lifted a brow. "Because you claimed me."

"My claim is all over you."

Before I could lean down to kiss her lips, the penthouse buzzer sounded, and at the same time, my cell phone and the elevator intercom rang.

"If that's your brother, I will punch him in the face. He loves to show up unannounced. I should ignore him and leave him standing in the lobby. Only those with the codes can access the elevators."

"He'll find some way to get up here." The sly smile she gave me said she'd probably do the exact same thing. "He's a Morelli, after all."

"Let me guess. Out of your siblings, you're closest to him."

"We're the misfits or the clan. We, the black sheep of the family, stick together."

I touched her ears. "You mean black diamonds."

"You noticed my signature stone. Impressive."

"I notice everything about you." I clenched my jaw and turned toward the doors leading into the penthouse. "One form of communication would have been enough. He didn't need to tag everything at the same time."

"That's Lucian. He wanted your attention."

I stalked to the intercom for the elevator. "Morelli, what do you want?"

"It's NYPD, Mr. Pierce. We need to ask you a few questions."

What the fuck could they want?

"Come on up."

Less than a minute later, the elevator opened with six officers. They all were bruisers of men who looked like they could take down a whole football team. This was overkill for questions.

They studied me from head to toe, assessing whether I'd run.

"Gentlemen, no need to bring a team to ask questions."

"We're here to bring you in for the questioning," The tallest of the men stated.

"For what exactly?"

A shorter, stocky man with red hair stepped forward. "Murder. It's best if you come with us quietly."

A throbbing roared to life in my head. Williams had finally convinced the cops of my guilt. No matter the evidence or the truth of the situation, he'd managed to make someone believe I'd taken Maria's life.

A prickle of awareness slid down my neck, telling me Sophia stood behind me. Of course, this was the last thing I wanted her to see.

"Let's get this over with. Let me get changed."

"No, you're not going anywhere." Sophia stormed toward us, fury on her face. "Do you have a warrant to bring him in? Otherwise, he is not obligated to listen to anything you say."

Before she faced off with one of the officers, I stepped in her path. "It's going to be fine."

"The hell it is. I know how this works." The anger in her dark eyes burned as if she'd set the men behind me on fire. "You don't have to go anywhere unless these men have a warrant. And we know Maria wasn't murdered. She took her own life. The words of a grieving brother would never sanction any judge to clear an order of arrest."

I stared at her, knowing, without a doubt, I'd never let her go. She continually stood up for me even when I knew I damn well never deserved it.

Just as I readied to tell the cops to fuck off, one of them said, "This isn't about a woman. It's about the murder of Keith Randolph. The fashion designer."

CHAPTER TWENTY

Sophia

"How long is this going to take?" I muttered to myself as I glanced at the wall for the tenth time and paced back and forth in the waiting area of the precinct lockup.

My mind whirled with too many scenarios imaginable, and the plausibility of Damon going after Keith for what he'd done to me wasn't far-fetched. But then again, not a single source I tagged in the fashion world said anything about Keith being dead.

One day, I wouldn't be such a fun topic for tabloid entertainment.

Now it left me believing either this whole thing with Damon was the cops' way of jerking us around, or Keith's family wanted his death kept under wraps.

He more than likely overdosed, and his daddy hoped to pin it on someone to save face.

I released a deep breath.

What would it be like to have parents who believed your word over everyone else's even when they knew you were a fucking liar? I couldn't even speak the truth and have even one of mine side with me.

At least there was one person I could count on to have my back in any situation.

Lucian.

When I'd called him, I'd barely uttered the words police and Damon when he informed me the Morelli family attorney would be waiting for Damon at the station.

I understood the rules. The less said over the phone, the better.

To my surprise, Mr. Sharpton had already started the paperwork and the process of representation before Damon had stepped through the precinct doors.

Lucian, on the other hand, had yet to arrive.

Where was he?

I gripped the back of my neck and continued to pace.

All of a sudden, I paused as a thought crossed my mind.

What if one of those asshole reporters who constantly followed me called my parents or reported this to one of the tabloid outlets?

One of them had to have seen the cops come into Damon's building. And that meant they saw us all leave to go to the station.

Fuck, fuck, fuck.

The last thing I needed or wanted was the Morelli crew descending in here like avenging angels and spending the next ten hours arguing with each other on how to handle the situation without listening to a single one of my opinions.

Lucian provided enough Morelli energy to demolish a building, then adding my father and Leo into the mix would send this place nuclear.

Plus, by the end of the day, I'd more than likely do or say something to cause more drama in an already powder keg environment.

I was giving myself a headache with all this waiting and pondering crazy scenarios.

On top of everything, my stomach felt like it would eat itself. My last meal was the less-than-stellar dinner at last night's event that I picked at.

Scanning the area, I searched for a vending machine. I could grab a granola bar or some snack to tie me over for a few hours. At least it was something to keep me occupied for a few minutes instead of this endless waiting.

Feeling my phone vibrate in my jeans pocket, I pulled it out and read the text message.

LUCIAN: *Here. See you in a minute.*

ME: *About damn time you got here. Do the parents know?*

LUCIAN: *Not yet, but it's bound to come out.*

ME: *How many vultures are circling?*

LUCIAN: *Only two for the moment. One of the fuckers asked me if I knew you were inside.*

I cringed. I'd guessed right about them following me.

A second later, Lucian walked into the waiting area. The scowl and utter annoyance on his face told me he'd used considerable restraint to keep from punching the reporter.

It also amused me watching some of the officers in the vicinity shift into alertness as Lucian's security positioned themselves in different areas of the room.

Subtle never entered Lucian's vocabulary. Instead, his style landed more on the in-your-face style.

At least the ones he'd foisted upon me had more discretion. They sat in seats among the other occupants waiting on people brought into the station.

Lucian caught sight of me and moved in my direction.

"Give me the details."

"There isn't much to tell you. They came into the penthouse in the guise of asking him questions and then said they wanted him to come down here for questioning about Keith's murder."

"I'll handle this. The whole incident is bogus, and they know it. They're after something else and jerking him around for another reason."

"How are you planning on handling this? A murder investigation isn't something you can 'handle.'" I used air quotes around the last word.

"I have my ways." His arrogant attitude had me shaking my head.

"I don't understand any of this. When did he die?"

"Thirty-six hours ago. Give or take a few hours." A look passed in Lucian's dark eyes that had me suspicious.

I tucked my arm into his and pulled him to an area where others couldn't hear us. "How do you know this?"

"Let me repeat. I have my ways."

"Please tell me, you didn't have anything to do with this?"

He narrowed his gaze. "Not everything has my hands in it. Besides, Pierce created the mess. Therefore, he is responsible for cleaning it up."

"You told him this?"

My gaze lifted to the doors leading to the lockup area for a split second.

Could Damon have done something to Keith?

A lump formed in my throat.

"This conversation happened last night. And between all the drama of the evening and this morning, he wouldn't have had the time. Then, also, there is the fact that murder happened before the gala."

A sense of relief washed over me, and more worry crept in.

"Then who could have done it?"

"You could figure it out better than anyone else."

"What gives you that conclusion?"

"You run in the same circles and can generate a list of enemies the fucker racked up."

"I was his enemy number one." I rubbed a hand across my face. "Why had I let my anger get the best of me? If I hadn't gone there with Lizzy that night, then none of this would have happened—"

"Hold up. You took Lizzy with you?" Irritation filled Lucian's voice. "You left that bit out in the retelling of your adventure. When you said "we," I thought you meant you took one of your friends with you on this idiot escapade."

I cringed, trying to rack my memory of what I'd told him. I could have sworn I'd given him all the details. Shit, maybe I had forgotten to tell him about Lizzy.

"I never left her out on purpose. I only gave you the important details."

"You took the youngest of us on a half-assed, amateur-style vigilante break-in and didn't think it was important information?"

"When you say it like that, it does sound bad."

Lucian crossed his arms across his chest. The vein on his forehead pulsed, and for the first time since I was young, I realized I'd pissed him off beyond what he could handle from me.

"I'm sorry."

"I don't want to hear you're sorry. I want you to go through every fucking detail, from what you wore, who you met, what you said. Don't leave a single thing out."

I swallowed, closed my eyes, and recounted every minute detail.

"Do you realize how much danger you put Lizzy in?"

"I know." I glared at him. "Don't you think I feel guilty enough?"

"Guilty or not, it was a dumbass thing to do.

How did she handle the aftermath?"

"She's fine. Baby or not, she isn't as delicate as you think. Yeah, she had that panic attack at Damon's, but I think it was just the adrenaline." I pursed my lips. "She swiped all the alcohol from my place to take back to school with her if that tells you anything. She's a normal college kid."

The crease between his brows told me he wasn't convinced.

"The thought of someone doing to her what Randolph did to you." Lucian clenched his fists. "None of this would have happened if you had told me from the beginning. I would have taken him out back then."

"I know. I was scared and didn't want his blood on your hands." I pinched the bridge of my nose. "Maybe if I'd been stronger and fought back or gotten one of you involved, he wouldn't have continued to harass so many other girls. He was such a monster."

"I fucking wish I'd been the one to kill Randolph with my bare hands. The bastard deserved to die."

"Will you be quiet," I exclaimed. "We're in a police station. You don't want to call out wishes of killing anyone, especially being who we are."

"Does this look like the face of someone who

gives a shit? Besides, he's already dead. Wishing I killed him doesn't mean I did anything to him. And for the record, if Pierce killed him, I'm glad he did. The predator needed to die."

"You just got through saying you told Damon to handle Keith last night, not over thirty-six hours ago. Besides, I know he's innocent. He may have beaten Keith to a pulp, but he wouldn't have murdered him."

"You're so sure."

"I am." I glared at him. "I know you're fine with it, so stop pretending otherwise."

"Fine with what?"

"Pierce and me."

He grunted in response, making me smirk.

"I'll never fit into any standard mold. That's why I get into trouble so much."

"You get into trouble because you don't conform to the rules of society, and you have this inability to listen to good advice from your wiser oldest brother."

I shrugged. "I won't deny it."

The doors in the back of the waiting area opened, and my heart skipped a beat.

When the officer who exited moved toward another group of people, the urge to pace again coursed through me.

"How long do you think we'll have to wait? I'm going stir-crazy. They haven't given me any information since I got here. Until you told me, I didn't even know when Keith died. I still don't know how he died."

"I'll tell you in a moment. First, let me see if I can get anything out of them. I'm sure I can convince at least a little information out of someone."

"Be my guest."

At that moment, Damon emerged into the secured hallway separating the waiting and interrogation rooms. Mr. Sharpton and two officers walked beside him, all speaking to each other, while Damon remained silent.

He wore his standard blank expression, but I saw the exhaustion shadowing his face.

Our eyes connected, and my heart clenched, that unexplainable tether we shared locked into place.

I was in love with this man.

CHAPTER TWENTY-ONE

Damon

I STARED INTO Sophia's dark eyes wanting nothing more than to stalk over and wrap her in my arms. But these assholes were taking their sweet fucking time, as they had with everything today.

Three hours of questioning to dissect every minute detail of the last forty-eight hours of my existence. Thank God for Lucian's attorney since the assholes were determined to get me to admit to a crime they knew damn well I hadn't committed.

Every time they came up with another way to ask me the same damn question, Sharpton interceded and put the fuckers in their place.

Half the time, I wondered if they thought Sharpton or I were stupid.

It was a colossal waste of time.

Yeah, I got that they were doing their job. And the two cops coming out with me weren't too bad in the grand scheme of things. They were just following orders.

The two dick investigators who walked in with their cocky attitudes, all ready to go to lunch thinking they had an open and shut case, were the ones I wanted to punch. The fuckers thought they could poke holes in my alibi and call it a day.

Too bad for them, my whereabouts were airtight.

It still hadn't mattered. They were convinced I had something to do with the murder, and nothing would change their minds.

If I planned Randolph's demise, I'd never make it so easy as poison. That was a total pussy way to make it happen.

I'd want him to suffer, wish for death, beg for mercy. I'd enjoy watching the life drain out of his eyes. And most of all, I wouldn't leave a body behind like some chump amateur.

Shit. I needed to get the fuck out of here and clear my head. After all these years of hanging around him, Lucian seemed to have rubbed off on me.

Then again, Keith the fucker continued to hurt Sophia. So I wasn't sorry, he was dead.

It was disappointing that I wouldn't get to enact my plan to avenge Sophia.

Come Monday, various news outlets and journalists would receive details on all the dirty little secrets Keith Randolph and his father went to great expense to hide.

I'd play a game of tit-for-tat.

The best way to handle people like the Randolphs was to give them a hefty taste of their own medicine. The added benefit of the public fodder would be what the unwanted attention would do to the family company's stock prices.

The door beeped, signaling the all-clear to exit.

Sophia stepped in my direction, but Lucian stayed her with a hand on her upper arm. The scowl she gave her brother would have made me smile in any other circumstance.

There was a fierceness on her face, which made me realize how hard she'd fight for me.

It was time to acknowledge the truth of all the emotions and turmoil roiling inside me. I stared at her as relief and acceptance washed over me.

I'd fallen in love with Sophia Morelli.

The woman took my breath away, even in this building with bad lighting, grime, and disgusting smells.

She deserved so much better than spending her time in this place. She should be surrounded by elegance and beautiful designs, all tailored around showcasing her beauty as if she were a priceless piece of art on display in a museum.

This was no place for someone so precious.

One day soon, I planned to have her wear the bikini of jewels she walked the catwalk in during fashion week. My penthouse of glass was the perfect place for an exclusive showing.

The heat entering her gaze made it seem like she'd read my thoughts.

Done with the insistent chatter between Sharpton and the cops, I strode toward Sophia the second I received the signal I could move.

"We're getting the hell out of here," I said to her when I was within a few feet of her. "If I never see the inside of this place again. It will be too soon."

Just as I reached out to cup her face, one of the cops moved in front of me, blocking me from Sophia. Lucian pushed her to the side, and I tugged her behind me. Whatever these assholes had in mind, I refused to let Sophia become collateral damage.

"What are you doing? I answered all of your damn questions."

"Why won't you leave him alone?" Sophia clutched my arm. "He's innocent."

"We know your boyfriend is innocent."

"Y-you do?" The tremor in her voice had me glancing over my shoulder.

Could she believe I had something to do with Randolph's murder? Well, it was plausible, considering my ties to her brother.

Lucian shifted, conveying he'd about had enough of the bullshit. "Then what is your problem?"

"We have another suspect. One with motive, means, and opportunity."

All the hairs on the back of my neck stood up, and my hand on Sophia's waist flexed.

"Who?" Sophia asked.

In the way her fingers dug into my arm, she'd drawn the same conclusion I had.

We both waited for the officer to answer, and then after an exaggerated pause, he lifted a brow and said to Sophia, "You."

"What? You can't be serious."

I turned just as the other cop who'd come with me grabbed Sophia's wrists, jerking her away from me.

"Let me go." Sophia thrashed in the man's arms.

The lawyer moved in the cop's direction and started arguing about rights, but my focus shifted back to the fucker who needed to get his hands off Sophia.

"Get your hands off her."

I was going to punch that son of a bitch in the face.

Before I could move, cops surrounded Lucian and me, forming a barricade around us and preventing any access to Sophia.

"What evidence do you have against her?" I asked while struggling against the two men holding me.

"We know about her grievance with Mr. Randolph and the dismissed complaint she filed with the fashion school about him groping her."

"That doesn't mean she killed the bastard. Listen carefully, asshole. If there is one bruise on her wrist, I will fuck you up." I threatened the fucker gripping Sophia's delicate arms like he planned to break them.

After everything going on, losing it at the station may not have been the best way to handle it, but at this point, I gave no fucks.

"Mr. Pierce, I suggest you get yourself under control."

"Fuck control. Tell him to stop manhandling her. She isn't a danger to anyone. He's three times her size."

Worry and tears filled her eyes. I had to protect her. This was my woman.

"Mr. Pierce is correct. The district attorney is my personal friend, and I have no problems contacting her about your use of excessive force with Miss Morelli." Sharpton's tone garnered no argument.

The shithead holding Sophia released her, and immediately a female officer approached Sophia, taking up position behind her.

Sharpton continued, "What you present is circumstantial. No judge would sign off on a warrant for this."

With a condescending smirk, another cop handed Sharpton a paper and said, "That isn't our only evidence. We have a warrant because we found Miss Morelli's fingerprints in Mr. Randolph's apartment. She is our prime suspect."

My stomach dropped, knowing there was no easy way of getting her out of this.

Tears streamed down her cheeks, and for the first time since I met her, I'd give anything to wish them away.

"Sophia Donatella Morelli. You have the right to remain silent. Anything you say can and will be used against you in a court of law." The officer pushed Sophia toward the lockup area and continued to recite Sophia's Miranda rights. "You have the right to speak to an attorney and to have an attorney present during any questioning."

I had to find a way to help her. The last time I felt this type of utter helplessness and fear was during my childhood. Back then, I'd been under the thumb of my sick, drunk bastard of a father. Now, the one person who meant everything to me needed me, and I could do nothing to free her from the hell she'd entered.

By claiming her, I made a vow to protect her. But I wasn't worthy of her.

I failed. My promises meant nothing when all I could do was watch the woman I loved be taken from me.

This wasn't where she belonged. Not this terrible place. Not with those bastards touching her.

I couldn't fucking lose her when I'd just found her.

I liked to joke about Lucian being unhinged. When I found whoever killed Randolph and pinned it on my Sophia, they'd understand the true meaning of the word.

✧ ✧ ✧

Thank you for reading CLAIM! Find out what happens Damon tears New York City apart to save the woman who's come to mean everything to him…

Want more family stories in Midnight Dynasty? They're ready for you!

- The owner of Violent Delights, Lucian Morelli in HEARTLESS
- Sophia's older sister Eva Morelli in ONE FOR THE MONEY
- Her secret sister Lyriope in steamy wonderland in KING OF SPADES

And if you're looking for more super-spicy kink? Then you definitely want to meet the Morelli's archenemy Winston Constantine in his modern-day Cinderella story…

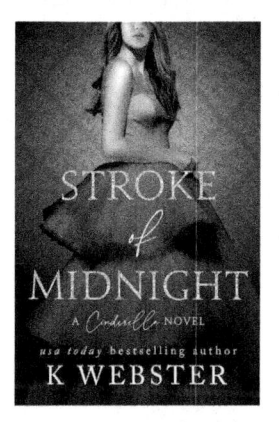

Money can buy anything. And anyone.

As the head of the Constantine family, I'm used to people bowing to my will. Cruel, rigid, unyielding—I'm all those things. When I discover the one woman who doesn't wither under my gaze, but instead smiles right back at me, I'm intrigued.

Ash Elliott needs cash, and I make her trade in crudeness and degradation for it. I crave her tears, her moans. I pay for each one. And every time, she comes back for more. When she challenges me with an offer of her own, I have to decide if I'm willing to give her far more than cold hard cash.

But love can have deadly consequences when it comes from a Constantine. At the stroke of midnight, that choice may be lost for both of us.

The warring Morelli and Constantine families have enough bad blood to fill an ocean, and there are told by your favorite dangerous romance authors. And you can get a FREE book when you signup for our newsletter. Find out when we have new books, sales, and get exclusive bonus scenes… www.dangerouspress.com

About Dangerous Press

The warring Morelli and Constantine families have enough bad blood to fill an ocean, and their scorching hot stories will be told by your favorite dangerous romance authors.

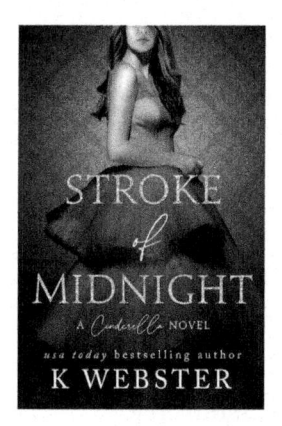

Meet Winston Constantine, the head of the Constantine family. He's used to people bowing to his will. Money can buy anything. And anyone. Including Ash Elliot, his new maid.

But love can have deadly consequences when it comes from a Constantine. At the stroke of midnight, that choice may be lost for both of them.

> "Brilliant storytelling packed with a powerful emotional punch, it's been years since I've been so invested in a book. Erotic romance at its finest!"

– #1 New York Times bestselling author
Rachel Van Dyken

"Stroke of Midnight is by far the hottest book I've read in a very long time! Winston Constantine is a dirty talking alpha who makes no apologies for going after what he wants."

– USA Today bestselling author
Jenika Snow

Ready for more bad boys, more drama, and more heat? The Constantines have a resident fixer. The man they call when they need someone persuaded in a violent fashion. Ronan was danger and beauty, murder and mercy.

Outside a glittering party, I saw a man in the dark. I didn't know then that he was an assassin. A hit man. A mercenary. Ronan radiated danger and beauty. Mercy and mystery.

I wanted him, but I was already promised to another man. Ronan might be the one who murdered him. But two warring families want my blood. I don't know where to turn.

In a mad world of luxury and secrets, he's the only one I can trust.

"M. O'Keefe brings her A-game in this sexy, complicated romance where you're left questioning if everything you thought was true while dying to get your hands on the next book!"

– New York Times bestselling author K. Bromberg

"Powerful, sexy, and written like a dream, RUINED is the kind of book you wish you could read forever and ever. Ronan Byrne is my new romance addiction, and I'm already pining for more blue eyes and dirty deeds in the dark."

– USA Today Bestselling Author Sierra Simone

One moment I'm the forgotten daughter of one of the most wealthy families in the country, and the next I'm the blushing bride in an arranged marriage. My fate is sealed in my wedded union with a complete stranger.

"A fiery, slow burn that explodes with chemistry and achingly perfect tension. Monica Murphy has written a sizzling masterpiece."

– USA Today bestselling author
Marni Mann

"Monica Murphy's The Reluctant Bride is a sinful yet sweet arranged marriage romance. I am in love with the Midnight Dynasty series!"

– USA Today Bestselling Author
Natasha Knight

SIGN UP FOR THE NEWSLETTER
www.dangerouspress.com

JOIN THE FACEBOOK GROUP HERE
www.dangerouspress.com/facebook

FOLLOW US ON INSTAGRAM
www.instagram.com/dangerouspress

About the Author

USA Today Bestselling author Sienna Snow loves to serve up stories woven around confident and successful women who know what they want and how to get it, both in – and out – of the bedroom.

Her heroines are fresh, well-educated, and often find love and romance through atypical circumstances. Sienna treats her readers to enticing slices of hot romance infused with empowerment and indulgent satisfaction.

Sign up for her newsletter here:
siennasnow.com/newsletter

Copyright

This is a work of fiction. Any resemblance to actual persons, living or dead, business establishments, events or locales is entirely coincidental. All rights reserved. Except for use in a review, the reproduction or use of this work in any part is forbidden without the express written permission of the author.

CLAIM © 2023 by Sienna Snow
Print Edition

Cover Photographer: Wander Aguiar
Cover Model: Thom

Printed in Dunstable, United Kingdom